JINXED

Other books by Thommy Hutson

Never Sleep Again: The Elm Street Legacy:
The Making of Wes Craven's A Nightmare on Elm Street

JINXED

THOMMY HUTSON

Jinxed

This is a work of fiction based on a story and characters created by Thommy Hutson and Catherine Trillo. Names, characters, places, and incidents either are the product of the author's imagination or are used fictitiously.

Any resemblance to actual persons, living or dead, events or locales is entirely coincidental.

Cover Credit: Original Illustration by Sam Shearon
www.mister-sam.com

ISBN: 978-1-944109-12-7

Published by Vesuvian Books
www.vesuvianbooks.com
Printed in the United States of America
10 9 8 7 6 5 4 3 2 1

UNCORRECTED DRAFT
ADVANCE READING COPY

Table of Contents

"Prohibit the taking of omens,
and do away with superstitious doubts.
Then, until death itself comes,
no calamity need be feared."
—Sun Tzu

"Break a leg."
—Unknown

PROLOGUE

The small private island was a mystery.

This, even when so many knew, or thought they knew, what was going on twenty-two miles off the coast of Seattle, on the strip of land named after the very rich and very dead Cadogan Trask. Protected like so much of the Pacific Northwest by Douglas firs, red alders, and bigleaf maples, Trask Island, a blister in the water, seemed mythical. Very little was known about the reclusive man who bought the uninhabited plot in the 19th century, later developing it to suit his tastes. His personal life and his purpose, just like his eponymous island, were ensconced in a thick, white mist. One day there, the next not.

Over the years, worry about Trask the place and Trask the man ebbed and flowed. No one dared argue that business on the island brought money and a small amount of prestige to the area, but there was *something* about it.

The same people who sang its praises also gawked and wondered and preached about whether its gifts matched its detractions. All of those armchair whatchamacallits peeked out the windows of their glass houses into their neighbors' glass houses and threw not stones, but boulders.

Always, always, they asked the same question: *Why must a high school be so private?*

The institution was nestled behind a wall of nature so beautiful that an equal number wondered how anything about it could be bad. A school for the gifted and talented. A place where children with an affinity for dance, voice, drama, art, and communications would be nurtured. A place where stars were born to shine.

But bad is a relative word.

And stars fall from the sky.

Still, the answer to the question on so many minds of what was really going on with those who were lucky enough, and rich enough, to find themselves hidden within its sacred *I hope I get in please God let me get in* walls?

Well, the answer was simple.

Secrets.

And not so simple.

Lies.

Spring, 1998

Trask Academy of Performing Arts was, indeed, very private.

The campus lay upon acre after acre of rolling green hills. Tall, age-old trees swarmed the landscape. Sturdy, dark red bricked buildings were scattered about. Cobblestone sidewalks—concrete wouldn't do, and asphalt was far too unsightly—snaked their way through and around the campus. Surrounding all of this flora, not to mention brick-and-mortar money, was a thick-ledged stone fence complete with wrought iron. The ornamental finials topping each spire had three-edged spear points. The borders weren't sharp enough to cut, but the tips were fine enough to puncture. And at only one point along the entire perimeter was there a gate.

One way in. One way out.

Down one of those lamp-lit walkways, in its own enclave, was

Williams Hall, a beautiful sandstone and cerulean tiled theater fashioned in a Romanesque style. A bell tower, now long out of use, still kept watch over the surroundings. The only modern accoutrement, though some would say eyesore, was the building's large, white marquee, added during the 1980s when, presumably, a faculty member, or perhaps a wealthy donor, convinced the school's administration flashing lights were all the rage. Its large black letters read:

52nd Annual Trask Academy of Performing Arts Showcase

Inside, rehearsal ran late.

The long fluorescent-lit hallway was filled with leg-warmered young dancers packing their bags. Actors filed away their scripts. Singers stopped their warbling. All seniors. Almost all rich. Wrapping up a rehearsal in the school's premier venue for the school's premier event.

Begun in 1946, the Trask Academy of Performing Arts Annual Showcase saw the best and brightest of the graduating class perform for a lucky invited audience. The theater's fifteen hundred seats filled with relatives, talent scouts, agents, bookers, managers. Hollywood and Broadway knew that those fortunate enough to study at Trask were groomed to be unsurpassed in their field, and what better way to find the stars of tomorrow than to watch the hopefuls of today. Rich daddies and mommies prayed the exorbitant tuition fees had paid off. Rumors swirled the cost to attend the school was as high as one hundred thousand dollars a year, which would make it one of the most expensive private schools in the world. For those prices, check writers expected nothing but the best.

And Hell hath no fury if they didn't get it.

Amanda Kincaid was working to be the best. She sat on the

stage alone, dressed casually in dark jeans and a top that showed just this side of too much. She was a pretty girl and, at nineteen, a year older than most of the other seniors. Her age made her more serious, and more guarded. Her dark hair, normally wavy, was pulled back tight. She wasn't a dancer, not really, but she felt the hairstyle made her look the part of a performer. Whatever part that was.

When she heard the last door of the night slam, she knew she was finally alone. She could now work without the worry of being judged by everyone around her. She was a good actress, she knew that. But that wasn't enough, and she also knew that.

Standing up, she grabbed her script. She promised herself that tonight was the night she would not peek at her lines. She knew them. She had to. It wasn't going to be like Showcase 1995—

> *Karen Reasmith stopped in the middle of her piece, mouth agape, spotlight burning down on her as if she were caught trying to escape prison.*
>
> *She had forgotten her lines.*
>
> *The adults in the audience, who could cut deeper than any razor, sat in irritated silence, while the other students lovingly absorbed the crash and burn before their eyes. A train wreck of epic schadenfreude. Karen looked around, helpless, hoping she could be saved from herself. But all that came were tears as she tore off the stage.*

Amanda thought of the joke around campus for those new kids who didn't understand how serious Trask pupils took their performing arts studies. They'd ask, "Did you ever hear of Karen Reasmith?" When incoming students answered in the negative, the upperclassman would respond, "Exactly." Testosterone high-fives and estrogen giggles followed as they walked away from newbies who rolled their eyes.

But Amanda understood what the newcomers didn't. Couldn't, at least not so quickly. Karen had blown it. She would never even get a chorus audition in a touring show. Casting agents loved to talk. And what they loved to do more than talk was gossip. By the time Karen had packed her bags and left the compound, her talent was already colder than the iceberg that had sunk the Titanic.

Except that the Titanic had survivors.

Amanda shook off the memory of Karen Reasmith and focused. Her tongue darted around her red-lipped mouth, preparing to utter chilling words as she channeled Euripides' *Medea*.

"In vain, my children, have I brought you up, Borne all the cares and pangs of motherhood, And the sharp pains of childbirth undergone. In you, alas, was treasured—"

Suddenly every light went out, leaving Amanda alone in blackness.

Even the ghost light's exposed incandescent bulb had gone out, which made her anxious. Amanda knew the ghost light was a big deal, if only a superstition. She was aware of the firmly held belief that every theater had a ghost. And not *Phantom of the Opera* ghosts who taught beautiful, young women to become chanteuses. No, these were simply the spirits, perhaps of performers long dead, who remained in the place they once loved. Perhaps the ghost light allowed them to perform their own works when no one was around. Or maybe they just liked to watch performances.

Nonsense, Amanda thought. *The light is there so we don't fall into the orchestra pit. Or something.*

Still, she didn't like it being out. Just in case. Of whatever frightening case might be out there.

And then the noise came. Softly at first, but building in volume. It seemed to emanate from the back right of the auditorium. It sounded like the moan of a dead person who most decidedly did not want to be dead. Like a zombie upon its victim, ready to sink yellow and black teeth into the soft flesh of a neck, tearing out tendons, arteries, a larynx.

Amanda's breathing grew faster, shallower. She felt as if she were standing in the cold, black reaches of space. Tiny hairs on the back of her neck tingled. Her mouth opened, ready to scream.

Amanda knew she should have been alone. And she knew she was not. But she stopped herself short of screaming. Instead she cocked her head as the ghastly voice grew louder, transforming into something else, like something off one of those cheap Halloween sound effects tapes. Her split-second shudder of fear gave way to the crack of an embarrassed smile, then annoyance.

"Seriously? Not funny!" Amanda yelled out, her voice coming back at her with the faintest echo. Her words stopped the not-so-sound-effect sound effect. "I'm trying to work here," she added matter-of-factly. She smirked. She waited. *I'm ready when you are, idiots.* When nothing happened, she took a step to her left.

"Dare you try to cross without the guidance of the ghost light?" a voice boomed. Amanda let out a small yelp. "Who can know what evils from the past lurk within these hallowed walls?"

Wait a minute, she realized. *I know that voice.* Despite the darkness, she moved in circles, calling out.

"If anything evil does linger, it's probably from your pathetic performance, Marcus."

She carefully shifted closer to the stage's left wing. As her eyes adjusted to the darkness, she saw she was inches away from one of the thick, black curtains that prevented audiences from seeing backstage. The material was moving, ever so slightly. *Who is that? What dashed away behind the barrier?* She had to know, needed to.

She slowly reached for the fabric and started to tug on it—

A reverberating audio feedback filled the auditorium. Amanda reeled, falling on her tailbone. Then, silence.

The bulb inside the cage of the ghost light came to life.

Someone had been right there. Not anymore.

"Oh, come on. Did I bruise your fragile ego?" she asked cynically. She got no response and decided she was over this game. She really did need to practice.

"Fine, whatever. Can you please turn the stage lights—"

They came back on before she could finish.

Jerks, she thought.

She looked back down at her script. Mumbling the words to get back to her place, she heard a rustling deep backstage. Hushed voices talking fast. Getting more strident. Urgent.

Inconsiderate jerks. Looking up, she projected to the back of the auditorium.

"In you, alas, was treasured many a hope of loving sustentation in my age, of tender laying out when I was dead—"

"Do something!" a voice said harshly backstage.

A female voice that Amanda couldn't make out responded, "Just go, just go!" It sounded like she might have been crying.

Amanda stopped worrying about her performance. She stopped wondering who was scuttling around. She was concerned that something was wrong. These people had laughed at first, but now they sounded worried. And very frightened.

So was Amanda. She stepped toward the left wing once again, this time with purpose. Something slammed backstage. Amanda screamed, threw her hands to her mouth, and let script pages flutter to the ground in a jumbled mess she would normally have cared about, but not now. Something was happening. Her expression turned to sour terror when she saw it.

Smoke.

Thick dark billows wafting up from backstage.

"Oh my God." She instinctively reached forward for the curtain, calling out. "Are you guys all—"

As she drew the curtain back, Amanda watched ravenous flames grow with a fresh gust of delicious, necessary oxygen. She was thrown as the heat slapped her body.

Crawling backward, she stumbled to her feet, turned to run, and screamed again, this time louder. She barely missed falling into the orchestra pit ten feet below.

"Help me!" she cried, looking around frantically, noticing the pages of her script dancing in a small vortex of flame, smoke, and heat. Flames licked the ceiling and rained dripping bits of burning material down. An ember from a set piece dropped to her arm, searing her flesh. She whimpered, hot tears flowing down her face. Another ember, another burn.

Desperate, Amanda tried to use her hands to wave away the smoke, but it was too thick. Coughing, she pushed toward a set of exit doors off the left wing of the stage. She imagined the fresh evening air outside, but her arms almost snapped when she slammed into the door that would not open.

For a moment Amanda wasn't sure what was going on, but another ember landed on her hair and began smoldering, bringing her back. She swatted at it, screaming. She got up and tried the door again. It wouldn't budge. She pounded on it.

"Help me! Somebo—"

Amanda violently coughed. She looked around, water in her eyes from fear and fire. The conflagration had engulfed the auditorium and Amanda, rushing to the stage again, realized she was at the center of it all.

A twisted, groaning came from above and, realizing just in time what it was, she scurried as a lighting rig swung right past her.

She didn't have much time. More and more fly ropes snapped

in the heat. Scene flats crashed to the floor. The glass lamp of the ghost light exploded. Disoriented, Amanda stumbled across the stage as smoke stung her eyes and heat filled her lungs.

Colored lights above burst and shattered, sending glass shards raining upon her. She covered her head, not seeing the snapped cable heading toward her.

It belted her in the leg, drawing a deep, thick gash and sending her sailing over the front of the stage.

Into the orchestra pit.

Her head hit the wooden floor with a crack. Her leg twisted at an odd angle. She was not going anywhere.

It's so much cooler down here, she thought sadly. The fire drew closer as debris rained down around her. She looked high above and saw fire crawl up the curtains, licking at the Trask Academy of Performing Arts crest. Its enamel sheen bubbled in the heat.

The fire upon her, Amanda felt her skin burn. She used her left hand to rub the fire from her right arm, but everything sloughed off the bone in large, bloody, sinewy chunks. The pain was excruciating. She had been sure, when talking with friends about terrible ways to die, that after a few seconds fire would have extinguished any sense of pain, or that her body would dull it enough to make it more manageable.

She thought how wrong she had been.

She felt every lick of flame as if a galaxy of the hottest stars were slowly stabbing through her. Her head lolled to one side. Her screams withered. She wanted to cry out, but instinct had its hold on her, and the heat she felt every time her lungs sucked in was too great.

The air itself had become a scorching hell.

She saw little blobs of dancing light as she held, held, held her breath. The world was just about black when another jolt of pain brought her back, as if a gleaming, hot needle had been shoved into her iris. While the blinding orange and yellow of one thousand degree flames ravaged her body, she saw nothing.

Her lack of vision was not due to the agonizing pain. Or the shock that racked her body. The heat was so great that her eyes exploded, like eggs bursting in a microwave.

The young girl with so much life ahead of her was as good as dead. A burning husk of a person. The unconscious fear of suffocating grew to be too much, and she sucked in a giant rush of heat that melted the delicate, paper-thin tissue of her lungs. It was a pain so much worse than breathing in water from the lake where she and her friends would go swimming. Long before she had come to this school.

As the little oxygen left in her bloodstream wended its way through her dying shell, strange fleeting thoughts crossed her mind. It wasn't, as everyone said, a movie-like assemblage of her life playing at breakneck speed. It was, simply, random moments. The first time she saw *The Wizard of Oz* and wanted to be Dorothy. Riding her pink bicycle in the grassy front yard of her house, yelling for anyone to watch her ring the tiny bell on the handlebars. Hitting her babysitter's older brother in the face with a snowball, upset and confused that she could make a big boy cry. Screaming on a roller-coaster with her former best friend, Shelly, sure she was going to pee her pants from laughing.

Then it was over. Her human light faded, faded, faded with one last thought.

The baby.

CHAPTER I

Present day

Silver moonlight cast a pall over the remains of the burnt, condemned theater that kept watch over the school campus. Even with a new, more open brick façade already complete as part of the school's very expensive renovation, the scaffolding snaking around and up its walls read like the twisted bones of a skeleton deep inside a closet. But that fabled darkness, coupled with its offer of shadowed cover from faculty, made the theater a prime location for itchy students to scratch their desires, test their mettle, and relish in stories that brought back the dead.

"Some say you can still hear her screams in the still of the night."

The voice of the storyteller belonged to Max Reynolds. He was standing in front of the building, staring up at it as he spoke. A senior with well-toned arms that stretched his tight, white T-shirt, he looked pleased with himself as he waited for a response. His structured, boyish face wasn't always smiling, but when it did, it charmed everyone. This was one of those times.

"Lame, lame, lame," said Layna Curtis. A sarcastic smile grew from her full, naturally red lips. "Let's be real, not only has that story been told before about a jillion times, it's been told way, way better." She sighed and pushed long dark hair away from her pale, pretty face and over her shoulders, feigning boredom. Inside—though she would never admit it—she wasn't sure she liked being there. *That building,* she thought, *is staring at us. At me.*

"Oh, really?" Max asked, goading her, snapping her from distracted thoughts.

"Totally," Layna replied. Clever and confident, she would play the game. She nonchalantly picked at the pills of her cream-colored sweater. Max stared at her, his eyebrows raised. Without looking up, Layna said, "Guys, am I right?"

Layna looked first to Nancy Groves, a fantastic dancer who was stretching her legs as if a loop of Olivia Newton-John's "Physical" played in her head. Holding her legs at seemingly impossible angles was par for the course for Nancy. She had a lithe body that shimmered when she performed. Layna knew it. Everybody knew it. And Nancy loved that. But Layna knew her friend's Achilles' heel was her short, bobbed hair, so naturally straight that even the strongest Ogilvy home perm would be hard-pressed to win the battle. Not that she hadn't tried, often with a lot of help from Layna and shared fits of laughter. Layna appreciated Nancy knew what she had and how to use it.

When Nancy didn't respond, Layna's eyes went to Alice Reitman. Alice smacked her chewing gum. She was cute, but nowhere near Nancy-thin. Layna had always thought that Alice wasn't fat. At least not fat, fat. And Layna knew that Alice despised in a *gag me with a spoon* way when people referred to her as "the bubbly one." That usually meant fat. Layna felt bad knowing most people openly said Alice was talkative and upbeat, but also thought the girl's blue eyes were thinking, *Thanks, now hand over the ho-ho's and you won't get hurt.* But what did it matter to Layna? Alice wasn't an actor, singer, or dancer. She studied communications and was going to be "the next, not-quite-as-thin Katie Couric." Layna had told Alice that was a fine choice, but she preferred Savannah Guthrie, even though she looked much taller than her guests, and it often appeared she might just lurch over and devour them. They all have their flaws, Layna reminded herself.

At the end of the line was Trask's "it" girl, Sydney Miller. Pretty, with blonde hair in perfectly placed waves, Sydney was popular and athletic. Layna admired her. At Trask, and in real life, Layna had to assume, guys wanted Sydney and girls wanted to be her. When she walked down the halls, the underclassmen all turned their heads to catch a glimpse of *the* Sydney Miller. If the singers were belting out a tune, they stopped as she strode by. Layna knew her friend Sydney was going to be famous. She had the talent to be a star, sure. But she also had a sheer force of will. Nothing was going to stop her from achieving her dreams. Nothing. And nobody. Layna admired that especially, even as she pushed down slight feelings of jealousy.

But like the others, Sydney just sat quiet.

Layna looked again at all of her girlfriends, incredulous. "Oh my God, backsies please. This is when my friends say they're *with* me?"

But none did. They stood stoic, staring forward, or around, or down. Looking worried. It didn't sit well with Layna.

"Layn, I mean, it is kind of a creepy story," Alice offered.

Layna's shoulders slumped. No backsies, apparently.

"Seriously, a girl died. Right in there," added Nancy.

Sydney leaned her body in closer. Layna could practically feel the girl's breath when she spoke. "It's just not something we should, you know, make light of."

Layna couldn't believe it. Her unease was giving way to annoyance. "Because some chick *supposedly* died in this awful, mysterious, tragic way a million years ago—"

"It's more like, only twenty years, but go on," Max said.

Layna glared at him long enough to make a point, and then continued. "I'm just saying, we see this eyesore all the time, but tonight we're supposed to all of a sudden be frightened because Max used his big boy voice to tell a campfire story we all knew?

Sorry, it just isn't work—"

Layna abruptly stopped. She had heard something. They had *all* heard something.

It was not the wind, Layna knew. Not the creaking of scaffolding. It was a low, hurting moan. A harsh, frightening whisper.

"Whooo—?" hissed the voice, from inside the building.

Layna's brown eyes went wide. Max sidled next to her. "Okay, fine, it's working now," Layna said. Nancy, Alice, and Sydney huddled close, too.

Sydney, worried, looked directly at Layna. "Dude, what did you do?"

"Me?" Layna whispered, too loudly.

"Shhh!" Nancy harped.

The punitive voice came back. Angrier, more strident. "Who wantsss—?"

They waited, breaths held, to hear what came next, but the only sound was the flapping of a plastic tarp over a pile of bricks. Then someone jumped out from the shadowed entrance of the theater. Layna let out a high-pitched scream. Then the others screamed, too. Layna grabbed Max tightly, trying to shield herself from whatever was coming toward them.

The screams of the others went on and on. And on. Layna gathered that something wasn't right when she peeked from Max's chest and saw her friends staring at her, their formerly petrified faces now swathed in knowing smiles.

"Whooooo wantsssss … a drink?" the stranger in the entryway asked.

Layna opened her eyes fully and unscrunched her face. She knew that voice. She'd been had.

"Come out, come out, wherever you are," Nancy joked, poking Layna.

Layna pursed her lips and nodded her head. "All right, fine, go ahead. Let's hear it," she said.

After a moment of silence, they burst out laughing. Layna put her hands over her face, embarrassed that she had fallen for such a cheap trick. Max pulled her close and kissed the top of her head.

"We totally had you," he said, then grabbed her chin so he could look her in the eyes. "And I'll always have you," he added, leaning in for a kiss. Layna greedily accepted.

"Get a room already!" Nancy playfully snapped. "And, Crosby, get your ass out here."

Crosby Williams' broad, white smile, and a glint from his hazel eyes, emerged from the darkness. Layna stared at the writer and part-time less-than-stellar illusionist, also a member of the senior class. She should have known—he could never pass up the element of surprise. He may have been lacking in the prestidigitation department, but he made up for it with a bohemian style and perfectly unkempt hair.

"I'd love to, but the spirits are insistent," Crosby offered. "You must come inside and face your fears, if you are to partake of the beers." He pushed his arm forward so it was struck by moonlight, waving a bottle that glistened with condensation. Then just as fast, he pulled it back and his smile, his eyes, and the beer disappeared all within the ruins of the old theater.

"You heard the man," Max said. "Duty calls."

Nancy, Alice, and Sydney moved first, with Nancy leading the pack. The girls laughed as they, too, vanished into the shadows, one by one. Max lurched forward, but Layna caught his hand and stopped him.

"Babe, come on," he said.

Layna looked up at the building, gazing at its two, large Venetian windows that watched over everything. *Watching me, I bet.*

"What's wrong? Let's go," Max said. "Or are you scared? Ooooh!" He waved his fingers in front of her face in a silly manner.

It broke Layna free from her worry. The small lie, one he'd never figure out, came forth. "Of course not," she said. "Let's go."

After one last look deep into the shadows before her, she gave Max a kiss on the lips. Ready or not, she let him lead her into the darkness of the auditorium.

The building was a far cry from the grandeur of its glory days. Gone were most of the plush, red velvet-covered seats that once filled the theater, leaving only an empty, sad expanse of dirty concrete. Those seats that remained, mostly near the stage and scattered up makeshift aisles, were blackened and charred, having melted under the heat of the fire. Layna felt a chill, even though the seating wreckage could barely be seen under the cover of dusty translucent plastic. Construction materials, tools, wood boards, and sandbags were strewn about, giving credence to the rumor the schools' deep-pocketed donors weren't jonesing to bring this part of the campus back to life.

It was an open secret on campus that the coffers of Trask Academy of Performing Arts might be drier than anyone in the administration wanted to admit. There was money, of course, because Dean McKenna knew that keeping up appearances was paramount, but there was an equally strong, although silent, opinion that the building was nothing more than a part of the school's dark past and, just maybe, it should stay there. Layna certainly felt that way right now. Neither she, nor her friends and fellow students, had any idea that in at least one of the more heated board meetings—old-boys club affairs always held privately with little fanfare—more than one donor had agreed: why rebuild a nightmare when you can construct a brand new dream?

Layna and her friends meandered through the maze of equipment toward the stage.

"All right, Crosby, come out, come out, wherever you are," Alice said, loud enough to cause an echo, but there was no answer from Crosby.

Layna and Max made their way to the front of the group. As they walked, they stared up through scaffolding and more plastic tarps, the former creaking and the latter flapping in the stiff breeze whisking through the empty structure.

Moonlight shone down on Max, who climbed up onto the stage from a set of rotting steps. "Watch the third one, it's a doozy," he said as Layna grabbed his hand for help up. Then Max, always the gentlemen, reached for the other girls, grabbing Nancy's arm a bit harder when she failed to heed his warning and her foot almost broke through the soft, pulpy wood of the stair.

Layna gasped, but Nancy just uttered an embarrassed "Whoopsie."

From the stage, the friends paused to take in their surroundings, illuminated not only by the natural evening light, but also by the lone ghost light in the center of the stage.

"Spooky. Maybe this was, you know, *the* light," Alice wondered aloud. The thought caused a hint of unease in Layna.

"Yes, most definitely," Sydney said with a smile. "Now let's steal the bulb and call GE so we can make a billion dollars on the light that lasts an eternity." The response put Layna at ease, but Alice rolled her eyes, blew a large, pink bubble, and sucked it back in her mouth with a loud *pop!*

Layna found that the light did not offer her any warmth, or security, so she just stood quietly with her hands in her pockets. Max sidled next to her and wrapped his arm around her shoulder.

"Hey, look," Layna said, moving a few feet past the light to where a picnic blanket was spread out on the stage.

Nancy went to it and stood with her back toward the darkness of the stage's left wing. "Fancy," she said. "Maybe next time we can have a picnic, I don't know, at the scene of a car accid—"

A hand suddenly reached from the shadows and whisked its way over Nancy's mouth. Unable to say anything, her eyes filled with fear and worry.

"Nan, how much longer do we wait?" Sydney asked. She turned and let out a scream when she saw Nancy.

Layna and Alice yelped as well. "Max!" Layna screamed, with the unspoken order of *Do something!* Max practically leapt across the stage. Then he stopped, and he and the others watched as the stranger's hand wended its way from Nancy's mouth, down over her shoulder, and to her jacket's zipper.

It started to pull down.

Nancy's wide eyes shrank to a disbelieving squint. She yanked hard on the offending arm and pulled a stumbling Crosby from the shadows onto the stage.

"Wow, way to be romantic, Cros," Nancy said. "I've always dreamed of doing it here. Literally, right here."

"Me too, babe. Me, too," Crosby joked, raising his eyebrows in quick succession before planting a kiss on her lips.

The others made their way over.

"Crosby, such a lovable jerk," Sydney offered, giving him a peck on the cheek.

"That's funny, I thought he was just being a jerk," Layna added with a little more annoyance than she had meant to.

Max crossed in front of her. "Me-ow." Now it was Layna who rolled her eyes. It hadn't been her idea to hang out in a burnt-out building, tell ghost stories, and do God only knows what. She would have been fine if they had never come here.

"Come on," Crosby said. "I couldn't let the ambiance go to waste. We're all entitled to a good scare, right? So, welcome children. And now, watch."

They all did as Crosby stood in front of them, arms

outstretched. He tugged on each sleeve. Nothing there. Suddenly, with a few slick gestures and a turn, he produced beer bottle after beer bottle.

"Well kiss my ass and call me abracadabra," Max laughed, happily grabbing two bottles and offering one to Layna. She shook her head. Max ambled off, saying something under his breath like, "More for me."

Alice brushed past Layna, smacked her gum, and grabbed a beer. "The party has so officially started."

Crosby saved the last drink for Nancy, sheepishly gesturing like it was a peace offering. "Forgive me, but in all honesty, I just had to set the mood."

"Oh, it's gonna take more than janky beer," Nancy retorted with a smile.

Crosby shrugged his shoulders, opened his jacket, and showed her the flask he had been hiding. Nancy's smile grew. Layna watched, enjoying their playful back-and-forth.

"You know me so well," Nancy admitted. She put her arms inside Crosby's jacket, moving her face close to his.

"And you me, my dear," responded Crosby. Somehow they seemed to smile even as they kissed deeply.

Layna cleared her throat and sat down on the blanket. "Tongue-wrestlers, your much-needed, very private room is now ready. Please check in, stat."

Nancy pulled back from Crosby, laughing. "Duly noted." She and the others joined Layna on the blanket.

Crosby remained standing by himself, still pretending to kiss Nancy. The others laughed, which he took as his cue to stop and take a seat. The teens kicked back, looking up at the star-studded sky through a gaping hole in the roof of the condemned theater.

"See, it's not so scary in here," Max said.

Layna thought, but would never dare say, that it was still just as creepy as she had imagined. Maybe more.

"Let's discuss break. Please tell me you're staying," Sydney pleaded, breaking the silence. Secretly she had also hoped to head off talk about the building, the legend, or how frightening it was. And is.

"Oh, we're staying the week," Layna said, adding emphatically, "All of us, right?"

Nods all around. Sydney let out a *Thank God* sigh.

"Rumor has it only D'Arcangelo and McKenna are gonna be here," Alice said. "And there's gonna be a party tomorrow night to kick things off."

"A freshman party, ugh." Nancy groaned and took a swig from the flask.

"I'll pass, thank you very much," Sydney said.

Layna looked like she was holding in a secret she couldn't keep in. "Max wants to go!" she revealed.

The group stared at him as if he were mad.

"What?" Max asked. "It could be fun."

Layna threw a *You've gotta be kidding me* stare at him. "Oh, totes," she said, "if the fifteen-year-olds can plot out how to sneak anything stronger than hard lemonade into the dorms."

Sydney shook her head. "Barfing kids and tragic pop music outside my door, all night long. Sign. Me. Up!"

"Oh, let me call the *wah*mbulance," Nancy laughed. "It's your fault. You could have lived with us big kids in Campbell Hall."

"Oh, no, no, no," Sydney replied. "I am not giving up my primo view for snot-nosers."

And it was true, she thought. Her view *was* fantastic, overlooking the conservatory filled with exotic plants, from rare orchids to ingeniously sculpted bonsai trees. Aside from the supposed eco-friendly gratification, the school's motivation for the garden was a mystery to Sydney, her friends, and most other students, too. Most of the kids at school, Sydney among them if she stopped lying to herself, had the mindset that if you've seen one flower, you've seen them all.

The beauty of the building, Sydney had to admit, could not be overstated: a dome of striking brass-capped cames that held together shimmering glass plates of blue and gold, the colors of the school. Sydney often found herself staring at the top of the structure, mesmerized as it reflected the setting sun. Beyond the dome, the rolling green hills that the school had so meticulously taken care of led to the thick forest just beyond the gates of the campus.

It was that view that kept Sydney in the underclassmen's dorm. She had lucked out with her room. The school used the stunning views and state-of-the-art facilities to lure new students, but after the main academic coursework was finished in year one, students started their majors and moved to one of two dorms on campus closer to the buildings where they would train. Still Sydney accepted that the spectacular view, and the slightly longer daily walk to her classes, was worth putting up with the kids who were just finding their way. When she had asked to stay in her room, the housing committee decided she could. Sure, there were moments when she thought it might be more fun to be in a building with all of her friends, seniors who had paid their dues and were ready to graduate and make their mark with the talents that Trask had nurtured within them. But when the committee said yes if she agreed to stay at the school for her entire academic career, she had made her choice.

Sydney was shaken from her thoughts of pretty stained glass and obnoxious newbies when Crosby said, "They'll be in dreamland before you know it. The last ferry leaves Saturday morning and they'll wanna be bright-eyed for mommy and daddy at the docks."

"Speaking of morning, like, what's with the ratchet, military-style early rehearsal, Syd?" Alice asked. "It's just us, and you're the only one in the showcase."

"Oh, don't be silly," Layna said, smiling. "The *star* here needs someone to shine the spotlight on her the minute day breaks, didn't you know?" Sydney wondered, for just a second, whether something more wicked lurked behind the comment and smile.

"Oh, the shade!" Nancy said.

"Guys, I was joking. Seriously," Layna offered. She took Sydney's hand. "Hey, when have I not been the overachieving understudy to the world's soon-to-be most famous talent?"

The words didn't make Sydney feel much better. Sydney knew how badly Layna wanted to perform. "Layn, you'll get your chance. Trust me, it'll happen."

"You're right," agreed Layna, "the minute you pull a Peg Entwistle and take a leap off the Hollywood sign."

"Layna!" Nancy laughed, half-heartedly.

Sydney chuckled slightly, then looked away. She didn't want to keep up the contest with Layna, didn't want to see something in her friend's eyes that might betray their friendship.

Max took a long swig from his beer and gestured at their surroundings with the bottle. "There's always hope for a mysterious fire during one of Syd's rehearsals."

"Okay, seriously, starting to feel uncomfortable here," Sydney admitted. She looked at Layna, waiting for the break. It finally came. They locked eyes, and Layna's big grin forced one from Sydney.

"Babe, friends to the end," Layna said, moving to wrap her arms around Sydney. "The very end," she added, her tone both playful and menacing.

Everyone relaxed as Sydney playfully pushed Layna away. "Girl, bye!"

The wind picked up, whistling through the theater. The scaffolding creaked and groaned. A light flurry of plaster dust sprinkled down, looking, Sydney thought, perhaps too much like ash from a fire.

"The universe likes the idea, Syd," Crosby said. "Maybe your number is up."

"And I like the idea of you shutting up," Sydney replied sharply. She had reached her limit on the subject of past deaths as well as jokes about her own.

Layna grabbed Sydney's hand and gave it a squeeze. "Sorry. I didn't mean to—"

Alice yelped as floorboards creaked in the darkness of the stage wings. "That was so not the wind," she muttered.

Max stood tall, taut, alert. "Who's there?" he asked.

No response. Layna grabbed his arm. He motioned for her and everyone else to be quiet as he stepped toward the edge of the light thrown out from the ghost lamp.

"Ooh, tough guy," Crosby mumbled, snickering. Nancy slapped his arm. Max glared at him and then disappeared into the shadows.

Sydney was worried. And that meant they all must be worried, she thought. Was that an animal? Was it a teacher? Or had something they mentioned too many times that night come back?

As soon as she heard the crash, Sydney stopped wondering and let out a scream.

"Max!" Layna screamed, darting to her feet out of instinct. The others rose up behind her. Nancy pushed Crosby forward. He cocked his head and opened his eyes wide. Sydney imagined him thinking exactly what she was thinking, *Just what am I supposed to do?*

"Do *something*, idiot," Nancy ordered.

Crosby inched toward the darkness, stopping at another noise, a scuffling, this time closer.

"Not necessary," Max's voice came from the shadows. Sydney was relieved as she watched somebody being forced from the wing and onto the ground. The other girls screamed, as did Crosby. Sydney took note that his scream was more high-pitched and went on a hair longer than the girls', which she knew he'd regret.

Max appeared again.

"What the hell are you doing here, you stalker douchebag?" Max asked whoever was skulking backstage.

Sydney focused on Layna. She knew what was going to happen next. Her eyes met Max's judging gaze. She took a sharp breath in and forgot the drama and worry from before. Max was obviously not happy with the person lying on the floor in front of them all.

Layna knew she could not hide what Sydney, what Max, what everyone saw as she looked at the heap on the ground.

Dillon Reeves. A loner and, some have said, a rebel.

He was also a senior, though the rumor on campus was that the musical prodigy might have been older than everyone else after being held back in grade school. It wasn't for lack of intelligence, apparently, on which everyone agreed. Depending on whom you asked, though, the true reason changed. Imaginations ran wild. And the stories got bigger.

> *I heard Dillon would just sit in the corner of his kindergarten classroom and hum after he got yelled*

> *at for eating cookies another kid brought, so they held him back.*
>
> *I heard Dillon took a broken paint brush and stabbed another student in eighth grade for making fun of his still-life art project, so they held him back.*
>
> *I heard Dillon got blamed for pushing his high school shop teacher into a table saw blade and then ran through the halls screaming the teacher was jumping around like fleas on a hot brick, so they held him back.*

There was also one about embezzlement, and some even whispered about a true murder. Layna hated that one and knew it was not, could not be, true. Still, on and on it went. The lightning speed of Trask's gossip train left some wondering if, after putting the pieces together, Dillon wasn't in fact responsible for the Lindbergh kidnapping. *Stranger things have totally happened!*

Layna believed none of it. Dillon was just special. Quiet, smart, very cute. Dillon's looks and charm and bad boyishness did not go unnoticed. Almost every girl on campus noticed, and some boys, of course. But it was all of him—the things she knew, the things she learned, and yes, even the things she did not know but hoped to one day—that had attracted Layna during junior year when Dillon had transferred in. This was before Max, of course, a time her friends ridiculously referred to as Proto-Max.

"Are you all right?" Layna asked, looking Dillon over and brushing off his dark leather jacket.

"I'm fine," he answered, standing up. He was tall. Taller than the others. Layna tried to hide the fact that she did not mind him looking into her dark eyes with his blues.

"I hope I didn't hurt his man bun," Max scoffed. Layna eyed

him with a *not now* look. Max rolled his eyes. She knew he was sick of this. Sick of Dillon.

The others looked on with fascination at the love triangle. Layna was keenly aware that her friends knew she used to love Dillon, who was always slightly aloof in his love for her, who eventually fell out of love with him and into love with Max. Thankfully, Max loved her back more fully than Dillon ever did.

Max backed away, saying, "Fine, then the party's over. At least for me."

Layna stepped toward Max. "Max, stop."

He did. But he didn't turn around. She hated when he talked to her with his back. "If you want El Creepo to make it through senior year, you're gonna have to make a choice."

Layna just stared at him. The others stared at her. Alice whispered, "She must be answering him with her mind!"

Crosby laughed. Layna frowned, but she took some comfort when Nancy rolled her eyes and elbowed her boyfriend in the rib. No laughing. Check.

Everyone watched intently, not sure what was going to happen next.

No one expected it when Dillon grabbed Layna's hand.

"Dude! Not. Cool," Crosby offered.

Max turned around with enough time to see Dillon's hand slink away from Layna's. "What are you doing?" she snapped at Dillon. She ran to Max and put a hand on his shoulder. Slinking around to his front, she faced him.

"Him or me, Layna. I can't play this game forever," Max said.

"He's just trying to get a rise out of you. And it's working." Layna knew it was a lie the moment it rolled off her tongue, so she wasn't surprised when Max called her on it.

"No, Layn, you were helping him get a rise," Max said.

Layna grimaced, wanting to scold Max for being so gauche in

front of her—their—friends, especially Dillon. But she wasn't fast enough.

Max sighed. "Him or me." He kissed Layna on the forehead then stepped past her into the shadows, down the stairs, and toward the entrance doors. All she could do was watch him. She turned to the rest of the group. No one said a word.

"I didn't ask him to do any of this," Layna said. She looked at Dillon. "And you didn't have to do that."

"You didn't have to let me," Dillon answered quietly.

"It's getting late," Sydney offered, moving past Dillon without a glance. She grabbed Layna's hand, and the two started toward the doors.

Crosby and Nancy followed. "Oops," he said sarcastically, bumping into Dillon's shoulder.

Alice rushed up behind Nancy. "Wait up!"

Alone on the stage, Dillon watched the group make its way toward the entrance. "See you tomorrow," he yelled out. "And I'm sorry."

Crosby, Nancy, and Alice exited as Sydney tried to coax Layna to leave. Layna didn't budge. She wasn't sure if Sydney understood, even as her friend walked away.

Layna knew Dillon could now see her only as a silhouette awash in moonlight. She watched him watch her. Her hair blew in a gust of wind that came through the open door. Fine dust particles rained down on Dillon. Were they anywhere else, Layna might have thought he looked angelic. Dillon shook his head, put it down, and then rubbed his eyes. Layna knew her time had come, that when he looked back to her, she would be gone.

She needed to be gone.

So she left. As the door closed behind her, she did not turn back. She wandered slowly toward Max, who waited for her. He always waited for her. That's what he did. She grabbed his hand,

and they followed the others back to the dorms.

But Layna knew Dillon was still on stage. She imagined him standing there, all alone, licking his wounds and staring with red, watery eyes at the ghost light.

CHAPTER II

The next day the bell rang in every hall, signaling the last class before the start of the break. Bathed in late afternoon sun, the campus was adorned with student-made signs celebrating spring break had thankfully sprung.

As vacation-starved kids filled the campus, those paper signs met their fate as students tore through them. They danced, sang, and screamed. They sprinted to the dorms to get ready for a needed respite off the island. Back to the mainland where life can be normal. Or as normal as life can seem for kids who are told they're the best.

After they throw their party on the island.

Deep within the trophy-adorned hallways of Charter Hall, one of the larger, more austere buildings at Trask, was what one of the faculty who hailed from Madison Avenue called the Wellness and Readiness Center. Thanks to an anonymous endowment, the structure housed a pool, showers, locker rooms, multiple exercise rooms, and enough equipment to rival the most elite training centers. The school had, in fact, more than one Olympian in its charge over the decades—something the dean repeated ad nauseam to the impressed parents of would-be students. In the real world, it was just a school gymnasium. Par for the course, though, the board felt that their institution was not only better than such a colloquialism, but far less crass.

So the Wellness and Readiness Center it was.

In one of the cavernous drill rooms, sweating in their white jackets and breeches, two black-masked competitors readied for a fencing competition. The slightly shorter of the two wore a red epaulet on one shoulder and made a final check of her equipment, making sure everything was in order on the garments built to withstand one hundred eighty pounds of force per inch. She then pensively rubbed the charm around her neck. A well-worn, gold four-leaf clover. Ritual complete, the bauble was tucked away as her competitor shrugged, waiting. It was time to square off.

The match began. The two fighters lunged, dodged, parried, and feinted, evenly matched in skill and speed. But the fighter with the red epaulet gained the upper hand with a fierce beat attack on her opponent's blade. Gaining priority, she continued assaulting the target area.

With the final point won, the encounter ended with the red-tinged fighter as the standout. Giving her opponent a playful swat, and channeling Douglas Fairbanks, Jr., the victor was clear. The loser, a none-too-pleased young man, took off his mask. Sweat beads connected on his forehead. He wiped them away with a towel.

The winner then removed her mask. Sydney. Also sweaty, she sauntered toward the boy, stared into his hazel eyes, and extended her hand.

"Better luck next time. Though I've said that before."

The young man barely touched her hand before skulking off. Sydney watched him, knowing full well that it was not the last time they would meet on the mat. Nor would it be the last time he would wind up the loser.

Entering the girls locker room, she looked up at the red glow of the setting sun beaming through transom windows. A few girls flew past her, all cleaned up and ready for spring break, giggling and chattering away.

Sydney sat on a long, wooden bench, took off her fencing outfit, wrapped herself in a towel, and grabbed a pink shower basket from her locker. As she tried to shut the small door with her full hands, one of her expensive shampoo bottles fell to the floor with a thud. Its echo reminded her that she was now alone. She picked it up, threw it in her basket, and went to the showers.

She entered a stall and shut the frosted glass door before turning both handles at the same time, a ritual that would provide the fastest jolt of perfectly heated water. As it cascaded over her face, she lathered her toned body with soap. Bubbles and water poured down her shoulders, her abdomen, between her legs, and she let everything melt away. Everything except the idea that maybe, just maybe, those girls were giggling and chattering about her. *Nonsense,* she thought. She was the most popular girl in school. She knew it. And they knew it.

She also knew that made her a target. What some wouldn't do for their chance to shine. But that was ridiculous. *I'm a senior,* she reminded herself. The year was halfway done, and in just a few short months, she'd be moving to Hollywood. It both scared and excited her. It invaded most of her thoughts, really. That and the showcase.

A door slammed. She gasped, gagging on inhaled water. Instinctively she covered her breasts with her arms, even though no one could see her through the glass of the shower door. But she could not see out, either. So she waited. Was there any other noise, or movement? Or was it in her head?

"Hello?" she said aloud, but not too loud.

Nothing. She looked around, easing up just a bit. Still, she worked fast to get the soap off. As her hands went around her neck something snaked down her back.

Her four-leaf clover charm necklace snapped under the force of her wet hair moving against it. Sydney watched as the last bit of chain sank down a wide drain hole. By the time she reached for it, it was too late. The necklace was gone.

"No, no, no!" she said out loud. "Dammit." The chain and charm were a gift from her great grandmother, who had said she got it from her great grandmother after she became fascinated with finding a real four-leaf clover as a little girl. Or something. It didn't matter to Sydney what the history was, now that it was history. She thought about going to see a custodian and asking if there was any way to get it back. Had she ever really even seen a custodian on campus? They'd probably tell her to grab a pair of fins because the drains went to the ocean. They'd turn and laugh or snicker at the stupid, pretty rich girl who lost her trinket. Bitch.

She'd have to explain this one to her mother, who was always telling her to take off her jewelry before showering, less out of fear of Sydney losing the jewelry than the thought of some bourgeoisie trying to steal it. As if people were going around yanking necklaces off each other. Rich people.

She wiggled her thin fingers in to the drain holes, struggling to get deeper, get more leverage. Hoping she'd be able to touch a piece of it and, by some miracle, lift it up.

Another loud noise echoed through the room. Sydney screamed and tried to jump back, but her fingers didn't fully retract from the drain. Her index finger cracked.

"Ow!" It wasn't bleeding, thank God. And at least her nail wasn't broken.

She stood, opened the shower door, pulled her towel around herself, and stepped out of the stall. Steam wafted out and met more steam lingering around the room. That seemed odd. She was the only one taking a shower. *Wasn't I?*

Another noise jolted her.

"Who's there?" she asked, trying to hide the hesitancy and fear in her voice.

The lights went out.

Her heart skipped a beat, caught up, and began racing. Heat filled her temples. Blood rushed to her head as she shuffled through the dark.

"Listen, whoever—"

The lights came back on, the familiar flickering and subtle tinkle of the fluorescents crackling back to life.

Sydney took a deep breath and went across the room to the sinks. Above each was a mirror clouded with condensation. As she wiped one of them away, something dark rushed behind her.

She screamed and thrashed around, throwing her back against the cool glass.

Again, nothing. Nobody.

Get it together, she thought. *Everything's fine.*

She started back toward her locker. Before leaving the room and shutting off the lights, she took one last look around.

Night cradled the nearly empty campus. A few kids rushed to their dorms, or their friend's dorms, guided by small, solar-powered lights adorning every walkway. From above, moonlight threw down its silvery gray hue, casting shadows as Sydney walked from the training center to her dorm. She kept a watchful eye as more and more students disappeared into doorways or behind closing curtains. She had been down this path more times than she could ever care to count, but tonight felt different. She wasn't just by herself. She was *alone.*

But not really. Off in the distance, someone emerged from behind a building. Sydney didn't stop, but her stride hiccupped as the paranoid thought that whoever it was could run to her, fast. Could get her. So she regained her step and picked up her pace. But the person kept moving toward her. Closing in fast.

There was no one else around now. Just Sydney and this person. She could see her dorm, where lights flashed behind drawn curtains and blinds. End-of-semester reverie. Sydney fumbled for her keys, cursing. *Dammit, don't look afraid*, she hated thinking. This was getting ridiculous. She was Sydney Miller for Christ's sake. She turned to face the walker. Stalker.

"Listen, Ass—"

There was no one there. Sydney looked around. She wondered what was going on.

Unnerved, she stepped backwards and glanced to the left, then to the right. No one. She turned to the door and jammed her key into the lock, where it stuck. Her eyes rolled as she wiggled the key and turned the knob, cracking the door open. Looking up, she screamed. A reflection in the glass. Directly behind her. Running. She spun around, terrified.

The stranger stopped and backed away a few steps.

"Woah, woah, woah! Sorry, forgot my key!" Some freshman girl. She wriggled past Sydney and inside the building.

"No prob—" Sydney started to say, but the girl was halfway up the stairs and not even remotely interested. Loud music, laughter, and yelling spilled through the door. The party permeated the air.

Sydney watched as the heavy metal door to the stairwell, with its tiny square of wire-meshed glass, closed with a substantial click.

"You're welcome," Sydney said sarcastically. She felt more on her own, surrounded by the sound of a party she was not going to, than she had shuffling across campus. She shook it off. There'd be plenty of parties, one day.

She heard a noise at the door behind her and turned to see what it was. Probably a student hoping to not-so-sneak-in to the dorm. But there would be no need for sneaking. Someone was already inside.

He was bigger than her, with a wide stance. And a mask.

The mask, made of silver and bronze, was a sickening amalgamation of the comedy and drama faces so well-known in the theater world. One half of its shiny silver surface was twisted into a sort of smile, one that looked gleeful after doing terrible things. The other turned downward, as if that same grin had melted away in pain and despair.

Nothing good could come of this.

"Who are—?"

He rushed toward Sydney, frighteningly fast. Shocked and confused, she felt his fist connect with her throat, hard. The impact shattered delicate blood vessels, bruised her larynx, and sent her spinning back to the concrete wall. Her head snapped against it, causing more pain and a momentary dizziness that brought flecks of light, like tiny sparklers, to her vision. Breath became a torturous mix of searing pain and the metallic taste of blood. She panicked, fearing suffocation, and emitted a tragic rasp. Crying hurt, but she couldn't stop the tears.

The stranger pulled a polished silver blade from under his dark overcoat. *Dear God,* Sydney thought, *it's actually gleaming.* The glare brought her back to cohesive thought. She had to do something, and do it fast.

I will not die here, she thought. *Not tonight.*

As he advanced, Sydney placed her hands flat against the wall behind her, making sure they would not slip. The cool concrete felt good against her skin. She locked her arms and, at the right moment, and with every ounce of strength she had, thrust her left leg high and forward. It connected with the stranger's chest and sent him staggering back toward the door. The force of the impact created a series of spider-webbed cracks in the glass.

The attacker fell hard onto his ass, and the knife slipped from his hand. It hit the floor with a loud clank.

Sydney ran.

Her legs were wobbly and her head foggy, but she made it to another door, grabbed the handle, and yanked it open. She knew she had to keep going, but she felt an uncontrollable urge to look back. The want—no, the need—to look and see if her attacker was down, or out, or both. She pulled the door closed behind her, then pushed her face to its glass square to peek.

Nothing. She looked left, then right. Still she saw no one. She used the moment to try and catch her breath. It stung even as relief flooded her. *I'm safe*, she thought.

Then the terrifying mask jolted into the bottom of her view through the tiny frame of the window near the floor.

Sydney tried to scream, but all that came out was a labored, breathy gurgle. It hurt like hell. She wondered if she'd ever talk again. Ever sing again. What this would do to her career.

She tried to tell her brain to shut up, to stop thinking of things that did not and could not matter right now. All that mattered was getting away. Finding help. Surviving. She felt the door handle shimmy in her hand. She knew she did not have the strength to keep the door from opening. Hearing the reverie above her, she made a decision.

She would let go. She would run. She had to.

She released the handle and used all the energy in her legs to leap onto the stairs. She grabbed the railings on either side as she heard the door fly open, hitting the wall behind it with a heavy metallic thud.

The attacker was strong. And angry.

Sydney's thighs burned and her calves flexed as she took the stairs two, then three at a time. Her forearms ached, her muscles cording as she hoisted herself up the stairs fast, faster, faster still.

She could feel the attacker gaining on her. The sounds of underclassmen and clinking weak, but still alcoholic beverages grew louder as she fought back the pain. She tried to scream, but it was no match for the noise behind the next floor's door. The party was in full swing.

Her hand slipped on the railing and she fell to the stairs, hitting her shin on the corner of a concrete edge. Her eyes squinted shut at both the pain and knowledge of what was coming next.

Strangely, nothing did. She heard only her heart throbbing in her throat and the thumping bass from the hallway.

Sydney fought back the pain of heavy sobs. Whatever had just happened was real. Now she just wanted to get to her room, call Daniel in Security, and eke out a few scratchy, painful words to get him to come to the dorm. He'd know what to do.

She used the handrail for support, making her way to the fourth floor where her room was. Everything would be fine as soon as she got there, she hoped. She reached the door and looked through the tiny window. Left, right and, yes, down. She even looked up. Nothing but the shadows of kids dancing around the corner. She opened the door.

The music blared. Gaga, maybe Bieber. Sydney walked toward her door, cracking a small smile, thinking the sounds of the bad boy pop star might literally make the whole evening worse.

She finally reached her door. It was fairly girly by teen standards, covered with streamers and pictures of her and friends at various functions. In the middle, just above eye level, was a large gold star, bedazzled with sequins that reflected specks of gold light onto her face. In the middle, in red glitter staring back at her, was her name. Layna had given this to her when it was announced that

Sydney, and not Layna, would be the lead in the showcase. Sydney thought it was too much, maybe even tacky, but she put it up anyway. She knew Layna meant well, and that her friend was truly proud of her. But she also felt bad that Layna wasn't going to get her shot. One senior star. One showcase. One happy girl. One definitely not.

Sydney heard kids coming closer. She wanted to get into her room where it was safe. Vanity forced her to think she couldn't let the other kids see her like this.

But then she thought, *Had it been a prank to scare her? A joke that went too far?*

Her eyes flooded again. Fear jostled her, exhaustion wrecked her. Sydney went to put the key in and noticed that the door was not locked. It hadn't even been shut all the way.

Her stomach dropped. Everything stopped. Her thoughts. Her breathing. Seemingly, her heart.

Revelers just around the corner grabbed her attention. She turned her head, just as her door opened. She didn't see the figure in the mask, but she felt the gloved hands grab her already wrecked throat and yank her inside the darkness of her room.

The hand covered her mouth with a sick taste of leather and salt. His other arm wrapped around her neck, and he snaked a sturdy leg around Sydney's lower half, trapping her.

Worse, she could only watch through her slightly ajar door as students drank their way into a conga line that twisted past. She hoped any one of them might peer inside a door that was open, but maybe shouldn't be.

A young girl with a party hat on her head, confetti in her hair, and a noisemaker in her mouth finally did. Bieber gave way to Taylor Swift as the girl seemed to make eye contact with Sydney. But Sydney knew she saw nothing more than a dark room and shadows. Sydney closed her eyes tight.

When the sound of the other students had filed past, Sydney finally opened her eyes. She felt the attacker's grip on her legs relax the smallest bit, and she thrust her right leg free, kicking as hard as she could.

The stranger's hold loosened in surprise. Sydney elbowed backwards, catching him in the gut. She felt a rush of breath on her neck, then he grabbed her again, threw her to the floor. He ran to the door and closed it. Sydney heard the click of the deadbolt.

He pulled out the knife. It caught a glimpse of moonlight reflected from a framed picture of the Bolshoi Ballet. Sydney thought, *I'm not even a dancer.*

But she could fence. As the attacker came back toward her, instinct kicked in and Sydney grabbed an umbrella next to her bed. This was her territory. The umbrella's reach was farther than the knife's. She charged with the metal-tipped canopy, nearly jabbing him, but he avoided the thrust. She charged, stabbed, dodged, and swung the umbrella in a frenzy, making contact a few times, but no real injury.

Sydney went for broke, grabbing the umbrella with both hands, like the baseball bat she wished she had. She swung at him as hard as she could, connecting with his shoulder. And then something unexpected happened. Something Sydney realized was one of the last things she'd ever see.

The umbrella opened. Indoors.

They looked at it, then at each other. He waved one finger back and forth, then he knocked the umbrella out of her hand. It hit the floor and rolled a half circle.

Sydney backed toward the window. Nothing left to grab. Nowhere left to hide.

Time stopped, like it had for Amanda Kincaid, the girl of stories and legends students told to frighten each other. And then Sydney knew. She knew.

At least there was no fire. Thank God for small miracles.

The end came in glimpses.

Gloved hands reaching.

Grabbing her throat.

Windows thrown open.

The room turning upside down as Sydney was hoisted off the floor.

She thought how it really did feel like floating when she was hurled out of her dorm window. She fell, face up, watching her attacker get smaller and smaller. The sharp pain lasted only an instant when her body broke through the conservatory roof. Shattered glass rained down after her, leaving behind a hole of twisted metal connectors with nothing left to connect.

Then she felt calm. Warmth encompassed her head. A darkness clouded her vision, which narrowed to a beautiful orchid on the table to her left.

Sydney's skull cracked open and blood pooled around her like a crimson halo. The fluid greedily filled in spaces between shards of glass around her body.

I finally saw inside the conservatory, she thought.

CHAPTER III

Bright and early the next morning, exhausted students woke up and rubbed the sleep from their eyes as the sun rose. They'd remember, mostly, the party from the night before. The loud music, the gossip, the drinking. But not much else. No matter, for all they needed to do today was drag themselves from bed, pack a duffel bag, and take a ferry to the mainland to see eager parents for a much-needed break. Their families would have too many questions, fawn over them excessively, and generally make too big a deal about everything their very, very special children did, are doing, can do, and will do.

It was a bit much for some of them. For others, it was simply never enough.

For now, though, the campus remained quiet.

The stillness almost translated to one of the black box theaters where rehearsals could be scheduled for the lucky few chosen to be in the showcase and work through the vacation. The performance space itself was just a large square with seating on three sides. The stage was elevated a few inches off the floor. The walls were a dreary puke yellow, completely covered with thick, velvety black curtains that rendered the room faceless, which was the point. That way it could become anything a performer desired.

Backstage were two simple dressing rooms, one for the boys and one for the girls, each equipped with makeup tables, chairs, lights, and racks to hang costumes. The ceilings in each room were constructed to dampen acoustics, with a sea of holes in the perforated gypsum tiles, an older method of sound absorption that many on the staff felt needed to be redone in order to modernize the space. Students couldn't care less, as it gave them ample opportunity to pass the time with a game as old as the tiles themselves.

A muffled thwack sounded as the tip of a red pencil struck a hanging yellow one, knocking it to the ground. The hollow sound of the cedar wood hitting the floor was drowned under giggles.

"Hey!" Layna exclaimed.

"All is fair in love and pencil darts," Nancy said. She was wearing a leotard and was sprawled out on the floor of the dressing room, her head touching Layna's. "One more and I'll remain the ruler of the universe."

"You have a very small universe," Layna said. "And for God's sake let's not talk about love."

Nancy wriggled and took the bait. "Ooh, is Lady Juliet having trouble with Romeo? Do tell, and keep in all the juicy, sexy details."

"You're going to be massively disappointed," Layna offered. "He moped for about an hour afterward and barely said a word to me. Whatever." She tried to sound cavalier, but she knew it sounded like the lie it was. She cared. Of course she cared.

"Typical guy," Nancy said. "But let me tell you, Maxi boy needs to think long and hard about trying to start break by screwing his only chance to get screwed."

"Shut up!" Layna shouted through a laugh. Nancy could be crude, Layna thought, but it's what made her Nancy.

Nancy threw her last red pencil to the ceiling with laser focus. It stuck. Three red to two yellow. "Ha! I rule. Utter ruleage. Call it, babe."

Layna cocked her head as if it would give her a better vantage point or change the outcome of the game. It did neither, so she just shook her head. "You must have had detention a lot as a little girl. And 'ruleage' is so not a word."

Nancy propped herself up on both elbows so that Layna stared up at her. "Losers weepers," Nancy stated. "Accept it. I'm amazeballs, and there's no need for further explanation."

Layna blew Nancy's dark hair out of her own face. "Just remember, it's not over until I get you to sing."

Nancy jerked back. "Excuse me, but I am not fat!"

The girls laughed. A knock at the door made them turn. "Please tell me you ordered a pizza," Nancy said, causing them to laugh harder.

Layna realized, again and again, that Nancy could cheer up anybody.

Max poked his head into the room. "Get yourself together. No sign of Syd. D'Arcangelo's giving her five, then you're up."

"Thank you, Mister Stage Manager," Layna said, trying to be perfunctory, even as she worried why Max was acting so workmanlike.

Max pulled his head back and shut the door. Layna saw that Nancy sensed the weird vibe between her and Max. She waited for her friend to do the cheering-up thing, but the door opened again before Nancy could offer any pearls of wisdom. Max peeked in, winked at Layna, then grinned. The door shut again.

It was all Layna needed. *Thank God*, she thought.

"Looks like the Capulets and Montagues are gonna be all right," Nancy said, grinning. "My work is done."

"Have you seriously ever read Romeo and Juliet?" Layna asked. "Max and I are not from warring families. And, spoiler alert, they both end up dead."

"I saw the movie, duh," Nancy said, "and what I do know is your relationship with Max is filled with more drama than Shakespeare could ever have dreamed up. But, rewrite, we'll minus the death thing. It's so tragic."

"You're a disaster." Layna looked at her watch, turning thoughtful. "Where is Syd, for real? She schedules this tacky, early rehearsal and can't even make it to suffer with us?"

"Stop complaining. It's not like anyone kept *you* up late." Nancy said as she raised her eyebrows playfully. "If you know what I mean."

"Gross me out the door," Layna said. "Spare me the gory details of your love life."

Nancy stood over Layna and offered her hands. "Just roll with it, babe. I mean, it's been four years of you standing in her shadow. Take the chance to play if she's gonna give it to you."

Layna moved to the makeup mirror. The bright lights showed her clear, porcelain complexion. She stared into her own eyes, and Nancy became a blur behind her.

"These magical people, who are supposedly going to make some of us stars, aren't coming to the showcase to see the understudy," Layna admitted. "But, for better or worse, as Mrs. D'Arcangelo always says—"

Nancy grabbed Layna's shoulders from behind. "What's your malfunction? Mrs. D. is a posh high school drama teacher whose own faded hopes and dreams for stardom were dashed after she didn't make it big in some soap opera, or commercial, or whatever. It's totally clouded her ability to see true talent."

Layna nodded. "I'm a little confused. Could you clarify your feelings on that, please? Come on, be nice," she pleaded. She really did like and admire the drama teacher's care and tenacity. "I really don't see it that way. And Mrs. D. treats everyone fairly." Layna believed what she was saying, even though she knew Nancy, and others, didn't.

"Fine, sorrynotsorry," Nancy said. "But, let's not forget, *dahling*. You are the scholarship girl. You have your own clique where money is no object."

Layna bit her bottom lip. *Scholarship girl. Ick*, she thought. "You make it sound like I'm Claire Danes in that Steve Martin film where he bought her, or whatever."

"I think Steve Martin is sexy! And he can play the banjo. All right, fine, you can be Julia Roberts in *Pretty Woman*."

"Um, no!" Layna protested. "And how did you so hastily take me from bored salesgirl—romanced by a suave middle-aged customer—to hooker? Although, to be honest, Julia Roberts was a pretty amazing hooker."

"I know, right?" Nancy wrapped her arms around Layna's shoulder. "But I see what you mean, so from now on you will not be the scholarship girl."

"Thank you," Layna said.

"You'll be the scholarship hooker." They both laughed.

"We will *not* be calling me that!" Layna made clear.

Nancy seemed resigned. "So you got a free ride. You earned it."

"I wish people would stop bringing it up," Layna said, downhearted. "That free ride is just a reminder I'm a poor, talented girl from the wrong side of the tracks whose mother died when she was a baby and whose grandparents somehow wrangled a scholarship out of this place." Nancy's eyes widened. "Wow, I am a total ball of laughs right now, huh?"

"Always, babe," Nancy said, shaking her head. She grabbed a piece of teal fabric from around the neck of an otherwise naked dress form, turned Layna back toward the mirror, and draped it over Layna's back.

Layna could only wonder what Nancy was up to as she tried to back them both away from a depressing precipice.

"I decree there's a new superstar in town," Nancy said, ruffling the makeshift cape. "Look! Up in the sky! She's young! She's beautiful! She's desperate!"

The gag worked. Layna turned to Nancy, their faces close. "You're a good friend. I want you to know that."

Nancy smiled coyly and slid the fabric around her own neck. "Oh, sweetie, you're adorable when you're right."

"Still, it's not like Syd to miss rehearsal," Layna said, then added under her breath, "or a mark. Or a line."

"Or, who cares?" Nancy wondered aloud.

"That went south fast."

"Come on. Once you're out there, people will appreciate what they've been missing. It's totally gonna be, 'Sydney *who*?'" Nancy ran her hands across the fabric before putting it back on the dress form.

"Note to self," Layna said, "do not borrow a pair of shoes from Nancy."

"And return them scuffed. Scuffed! Seriously, who does that?" Nancy asked, now serious. "Sydney Miller, *the* Sydney Miller, Queen Bee Sydney Miller, that's who."

Layna looked her in the eye. "They're *shoes*."

Nancy was preoccupied with the dress form and simply nodded. "Thank God you get it."

Max knocked and popped his head in the door.

"Hello, sailor," Nancy said, putting her arm around the dress form.

Max grinned, then turned to Layna. "Looks like you're up."

"No word?" Layna asked. Max shook his head. Layna cast a concerned glance toward Nancy, who simply motioned with her head toward the stage.

"All right, then. Wish me luck," Layna said.

Nancy rubbed Layna's shoulder. "You don't need it. Now go show Mrs. D. you earned that free ride."

Layna smiled, but it faded as she looked to Max.

"You okay?" he asked.

"Yeah, I'm fine." She lied. She wasn't fine. She had doubts. She wanted to know if she could pull off the performance. Was this really her shot? Did she truly deserve it?

But more than anything she wanted to know why her friend had not shown up.

Sydney's body was found later that day.

Not by any student, most of whom had left campus or were waiting on the docks to do so. It was discovered by a member of the custodial staff that Sydney thought didn't exist.

Had anyone been able to see, they would have witnessed an older Chinese man, a member of the greens department, unlock the door to the conservatory and enter with a bucket of fertilizer and a hose. They'd have noticed him filling the bucket with water to create a food mixture for the exotic plants. And they'd have seen him wonder at a small shard of glass on the ground as it reflected direct sunlight from above.

Like every other employee of the school, the sweet Chinese man in the gray coveralls had signed a strict confidentiality clause about what he saw and heard. As he noticed the glass and looked up, bucket in his hand, his eyes widened at the sight of the shattered ceiling and twisted metal. His gaze returned to the floor, and he leaned forward, peering around a table filled with orchids. His mouth dropped open as he let go of the bucket, which hit the expensive, marble floor with a thud, tilting on its side, its chemical contents oozing out. He peered through the delicate white petals of the flowers and saw the pool of blood surrounding Sydney's twisted body. He took a tentative step forward and saw the girl's head lolled to one side, with its ashen face and wide-open eyes.

The nice man with a kind face and a wife on the mainland screamed at a pitch higher and louder than should have been possible.

And then he passed out.

It didn't take long for school officials to converge on the conservatory and then Sydney's room. And that swiftness was matched by how fast it was decided to keep things hush-hush. The Chinese man had been worried that he would be fired when he came to and reported the grisly mess to security, but he was told to take a week off, with pay. And to keep his mouth shut.

Two privately hired, nondescript paramedics wordlessly tended to the body in the conservatory. No yellow tape. No fanfare. Not even a marked emergency vehicle. The paramedics were instructed to take the necessary photographs, deliver the camera's memory card to the school, remove the body, clean up, and leave.

The school had already inquired about having a forge master and glazier come to repair the damage to the conservatory's magnificent metal and glass. But, those craftsmen were with absolute certainty to come next week.

In the hallway outside Sydney's room, there was considerably more activity. Leading the charge was Alfred Parker, a plainclothes detective in his mid-thirties, from the mainland. Although his build was slight, he was strong and handsome. And he was serious. If there was an answer, he would find it. And in his mind, there was always an answer. He ran a hand through a short-cropped head of prematurely salt-and-pepper hair.

Parker was escorted from the hallway into Sydney's room by Trask's head of campus security, Daniel Henderson, who explained to Parker that he was a recent graduate from Oregon, eager to take his first assignment in some sort of law enforcement that didn't require him to pull a gun on a kid from the wrong side of the tracks. Daniel talked about having seen too many stories where, even if the shooter was able to walk away scot-free after the investigation, it was not without considerable damage to his reputation or the community he ultimately had to leave. Parker listened. Such considerations, he thought, made Daniel seem almost too serious about his job.

Daniel stopped talking, and Parker stopped listening, as they brushed past a nearby photographer. The young woman, also from security but not a resident on campus, was snapping photos. *A lot of photos all bound to end up locked away with all of the school's other secrets*, Parker thought.

"I'd like copies of those when you have them," Parker said in her direction. She stopped and looked up, but not at Parker. Daniel nodded, and she continued.

"We'll get them to you," Daniel offered.

"What about the students?" Parker asked.

"Most have already made it to the mainland," Daniel said. "The rest took the late run and should be docking soon. I have to confirm who, but there are only a handful of students staying on campus."

Parker rubbed the back of his neck with a cool hand. "I never thought I'd say it, but thank God for spring break."

The flash of more pictures made Parker squint. Fully inside the room, he could see it didn't reveal much. A teenager's messy enclave and an open window. He noticed a framed photo of Sydney on an oak desk.

"So young. So pretty," Parker said, mostly to himself, as he made his way to the window. He looked out and down to the shattered glass dome of the conservatory. Sydney's body, the blood, and the glass were already gone. Parker shook his head, lamenting the speed with which things were cleaned.

"Seven years bad luck, huh?" Daniel said, pointing to the open umbrella next to the bed.

"That's breaking a mirror," Parker corrected. He looked around the room and sighed.

"Are we boring you, detective?" a man's voice asked from the doorway.

Parker turned, and the silhouette of a tall, thin man entered the room.

Daniel stepped forward. "Dean McKenna, we were just wrapping up."

Parker cautiously regarded the sixty-six-year-old Dean of Students. He knew that the man had no plans to retire anytime soon, or at all, if it were up to him. The board was happy with his ability to keep students in line, deliver results to parents, and keep the money on the far side of the black. His motto was to lean on the rod because every child is spoiled, for he was one of the spoiled children a long, long time ago. His family was old money.

"Detective, may we speak outside?" McKenna asked, not offering a hand or stepping any farther into the room. Daniel looked at Parker as if he had better listen to the dean. Parker did so, not because he respected the man, but out of professional courtesy.

McKenna stepped into the hall, and Parker followed. McKenna eyed the door. Parker took the cue and shut it.

"Alfred Parker. The one in charge," McKenna stated with a smirk.

Parker answered with a closed-mouth smile. The dean could really be an ass when he wanted to be.

"Dean, thank you for coming here. I know it isn't usual—"

McKenna waved a pale, veiny hand. "This is not an alumni luncheon," he uttered. "How much longer do you need to be here? The faster we put this poor girl's tragedy behind us, all the better."

Parker replied, coolly, "It would've been more helpful had I been given more time to look things over and—"

"Figure out why this happened?" the dean finished. "These young adults are under far more pressure than most. From the school, but also from home."

"Something for the brochure," Parker said.

"Alfred—" the dean started.

"Detective," Parker said, pleased to do his own interrupting.

McKenna blanched for the slightest of moments, but recovered and continued more tersely. "There are a few hundred students on this campus, each one here to be judged, not just to be good, but to be the best. The competition never ends. It will cause cracks in even the most sturdy. Coupled with adolescence, what can one expect? You see it as tragic. Others claim it is the price of chasing fame and, for the lucky few, fortune."

Parker was visibly agitated. "Well then, it sounds like you have it all figured out. Kids so stressed they party themselves to death?"

"Exams are done. Spring break is here. Perhaps in their excitement some pushed a tad too far," McKenna said. "There is nothing malicious in that."

"I'm told a few students did not leave the island," Parker clarified.

"Seniors," McKenna said with an odd sense of pride. "Allowed to stay if they wish and prepare for the showcase. It is a rather big event for us here. People, important people, come in from all over."

Parker pressed on. "What about faculty?"

McKenna seemed to be getting bored. "Just myself and Lillian D'Arcangelo. She teaches drama and acts as a counselor, and the students love her. We live here on campus. And you have met Daniel. He watches over us all. I know you are terribly busy, but I must ask again, when are you leaving?"

"I'll be done when I'm done. And now, if you'll excuse me, Harlan."

Parker opened the door to Sydney's room and entered. He closed it behind him, leaving Harlan McKenna to stare at the star shimmering with the name of his dead student.

Max shifted on the concrete bench outside the theater where Sydney was supposed to have rehearsed. He and Nancy played rummy, but his concentration broke each time he heard Alice pop her gum. He gave her a look. Crosby lay on the ground, a long blade of grass between his teeth, and stared at the sky, flipping a coin between and over each of his fingers.

"I thought she did pretty good," Nancy said. "Not that I thought she wouldn't."

Alice popped another bubble and smacked her gum as she spoke. "Please, you know you thought she'd bite it." Max gave her another look. *The* look: *give it a rest.*

"You can tell her how you think I feel when she comes out here, how about that?" Nancy said, reaching for Alice's next bubble. The gum stuck to her finger, and she pulled back, grabbing the wad from Alice's mouth and sticking it in her own. Everyone groaned.

"You know she kisses you with that mouth," Max said to Crosby. "You might as well make out with Alice."

Crosby smiled. "Sign me up. There's enough of me to go around. Keep it in the family, you know."

"I'm good, thanks," Alice offered, shaking her head.

"Eat your dirt," Nancy added, snatching the grass from Crosby's mouth.

"Anyway," Max said, "word on the street is the party last night was kinda close to amazeballs. Gotta give grade nine props."

Crosby snapped his fingers in support. "Shattering the conservatory is an A-List event in my book, freshman or not. Glass was everywhere."

"A little birdie told me your plans to make a cameo were vetoed when you went all agro on Dillon," Nancy said, batting her eyelashes at Max.

Max gave her a weak smile. It hid his annoyance at the mention of Dillon.

"Who knows what really happened," Alice said before turning her attention to Crosby. "And just how do you know glass was everywhere?"

Max wondered the same thing. Crosby just rolled his eyes. Which was not an answer at all, Max thought.

Alice looked at Nancy suspiciously.

"Darling, believe me, Cros was occupied," Nancy said.

Max shook his head and laughed.

"All night long?" Alice asked.

Crosby got up and sat next to Nancy. He planted a heavy, wet kiss on her face, looking at Alice while he did. "More than Lionel Ritchie, baby." He turned back to Nancy and began tongue-wrestling.

"Gross," Alice said. "Well, that conservatory was like their baby. The Dean's totally gonna kill whoever trashed it. Seriously dead."

Nancy pulled away from Crosby, a thin line of saliva breaking between their lips. "Thank you, Katie Couric."

Alice cocked her head. "Anchorwoman shade. I know you tried it."

Max's attention was elsewhere. He noticed Layna finally stepped out from the theater and stood in its lobby. But she wasn't alone. With her was Mrs. D'Arcangelo, her mane of wild dark hair held up with a white sash.

The conversations dimmed. Max watched with interest as the teacher embraced Layna, who seemed to fall into the woman's arms with resignation. He could tell that Mrs. D'Arcangelo's gesture was designed to give Layna strength, but it seemed as if no hug could have been enough.

Something is wrong, Max thought. "I'll be right back," he said to the others and got up.

"There he goes, the fastest man on three legs." Crosby laughed.

Max stopped for a second to glare at him.

Nancy stared at Crosby. "TMI, babe."

"The dorm showers have their perks," Crosby offered.

"I don't get it," Alice said, looking perplexed.

"Come on, I'll show you," Crosby answered.

Nancy laughed. "Will you stop!" She playfully swatted his legs.

"You're all crazy, and we're done," Max joked. "I'll be right back."

He stepped toward the theater as D'Arcangelo exited the lobby. She moved with purpose, then slowed when Max raised his arm in a half-hearted wave. The drama teacher gave a slight nod, then put her head down and continued on her way.

"Okayyy," Max said aloud.

Max stood close to Layna. "Babe, what's wrong?"

Layna began crying. Max hugged her. He could see she wasn't ready to talk, so he put his arm around her and walked her back toward their friends.

"Isn't there a statute of limitations on the amount of making up you can do?" Crosby asked.

Max didn't answer. He was too worried about Layna.

Nancy slowly shook her head, concerned. "I'm not sure that's what this is."

Max looked into Layna's red, watery eyes. "Layn, you're scaring me." He squeezed her hand, hoping to reassure her. "I'm sure you did just fine. Forget what D'Arcangelo thought."

"She's dead," Layna uttered.

"What? Dead? Who's dead?" Crosby blurted out.

The others looked on with the same morbid curiosity.

Max was confused. "Babe, what're you talking about? We just saw her leave the lobby. Strange as ever."

Layna sniffled and wiped her nose on her sleeve. She swallowed deep, sucked in a breath. "Sydney. Sydney is *dead*."

Max felt his stomach drop. "What? What're you talking about?"

"No freaking way!" Alice stated.

A cacophony of questions erupted:

What happened?

What are you talking about?

We just saw her!

Are you sure?

Layna pulled away from Max. "I'm gonna be sick!" she said.

And she was.

Nancy rushed to Layna, bent over, and held her hair as she vomited up a runny puddle of egg and orange juice.

The morning, Max thought, that Layna understudied for a dead friend.

Parker had seen Sydney's body and the location of deadly impact in the conservatory, and he was left with an uneasy feeling. Especially after his encounter with Dean McKenna. There were to be no minced feelings about the man. Parker did not like him.

As for Daniel, who had gone with Parker back to the conservatory, Parker wasn't exactly enamored of the security guard's abilities. Still, it seemed evident the young man had a good heart, a good head on his shoulders, and a willingness to do what Parker needed him to. That was important. Parker wanted to be left alone on this, and he knew the school administration was going to poke its nose in wherever and whenever it could.

He surveyed his surroundings, both admiring and loathing them. The stone wall that seemed to go on and on. The fence, smaller than the main gate and made of black metal plates, closed. Taking a few steps toward the wall, Parker pulled out his cell phone and dialed. When nothing happened, he took the phone from his ear and grunted.

"Forget it," Daniel said, closing a small notepad he was writing in.

"When you said no service earlier," Parker replied, "I thought you meant in the dorms."

Daniel smiled. "No, the island. There are no towers here, and we don't pick up signal from the mainland."

Parker grimaced. "Great."

"It's all a part of the school's mission to immerse the students in a sea of learning," Daniel said. "The Dean has the only residence here. Other faculty and students stay in dorms. School owns from shore to shore."

Parker cocked his head.

"It's kind of nice, I think," Daniel went on. "Kids today are too connected. Brings back the good old days, in a way."

"Sure," Parker said. The good old days for Daniel probably meant DSL. Parker continued to survey the expansive campus. Perfectly manicured lawns. Well-managed buildings. A place for everything and everything in its place. "A suicide and a secluded private school. Film at eleven."

"What?" Daniel wondered.

"Nothing." Parker smiled. "Just the good old days."

CHAPTER IV

The campus commons, usually a frenzy of activity when classes were in session, was empty. Most of the blue, orange, and yellow chairs were tipped upside down on cafeteria tables. Vending machines reflected the rusty colors of dusk. At the soda fountain, which was free of charge to students, Alice topped off a Coke with very little ice, put the lid on, and sauntered over to a table where her friends sat.

Layna, who looked much better after a warm 7-Up and half a sandwich, pushed crusts of bread around on a plate in front of her. Max rubbed her back. Crosby and Nancy sat opposite them, huddled in a booth.

Alice sat at the head of the table so she could see everyone. Layna watched as she put her drink down and then her keys. Or, rather, her keychain, a fluffy, white cat that thunked when it hit the table. Layna thought it was cute but odd, as it was bigger than the two keys it held. She stared at it as Alice rubbed the cat's fur and said, "Sorry, but suicide? Really?"

"I just can't believe it," Nancy said to no one in particular, though Layna caught a small glimpse her way.

"Maybe she was depressed," Crosby offered. Layna could tell he was trying to sound firm, but she simply hoped the conversation would end sooner than later.

Alice smacked her gum. "No. No, she'd have said something. If anyone was an open book, it was Syd."

Layna played with the food on her plate. She wasn't in the

mood for this kind of talk, not now. Maybe not ever. She glanced at Max, who at a time like this usually had nothing to say. True to form, he said nothing.

Looking right at Alice, Nancy said, "Evidently you didn't read the chapter where she kills herself."

Alice scrunched up her face. "Eww."

It was now more than Layna could handle. "Can we just give it a rest?" It came out more harshly than she meant it to, but she meant it.

"Come on, babe," Max said, breaking his silence as he rubbed Layna's back.

Layna was having none of it. She shrank away, smirked, and made a noise that told him *don't touch me right now.*

"Hey," Max said, trying to look at her.

Layna pushed her chair back and addressed all of them. "Forgive me, but what am I supposed to do? To say? How do you want me to act right now?" She lashed out, or what she guessed was her version of such a thing. She was sad, hurt, and annoyed. This moment was certainly not on her calendar today. Or ever. She looked around at her friends, who waited for an answer she knew would not come. She hoped one of them might say something to help her muddle through.

They didn't.

"Then I'll break it down for you," she resumed, "because it's apparently very simple. I was told the bad news is that your friend killed herself. But on the bright side, congratulations, you're the new star of the Senior Showcase. Isn't that great?"

"You didn't ask for this to happen," Max said. "No one did."

"Really? I'm pretty sure I complained enough to Syd, to you guys, about not getting my chance. And then last night I said—"

She stopped herself and shook her head. She didn't want to remember. She took both hands and used them to push her hair back. She held it behind her head, stretching it out so the roots tugged at her forehead.

"You said, like, you'd only get your chance if she jumped off a building," Alice offered.

Everyone stared at her.

Layna pulled her hands down and hit the table with her palms. It startled everyone. "I didn't mean it like that!"

Alice mumbled, "Tell that to Syd."

Layna focused her open-mouthed stare toward Alice. *Really*?

Nancy hit Alice in the arm, hard. "Shut up, mouth breather. Suck much, or what?"

Alice rubbed her arm and made a face back at Nancy, who only rolled her eyes.

Crosby tried to head off any more drama. "Layna, it's not you. Not in a million years. We know that." He paused and took a small breath.

Even as the words started to come out of his mouth, Layna knew what they were going to be and dreaded them. Partly because it felt wrong. But also because she, too, had thought it. Maybe deep down, in a place she could one day bury and forget.

"But," Crosby went on, "I'm sorry to say, opportunity can come at a bad time. And it's okay to answer the door."

No one replied. Layna felt a pang of horror in the notion, but the looks on her friend's faces signaled he was right. She folded her arms. She needed to be moving, doing something. Anything. "Yeah, well, I'm meeting with McKenna and Mrs. D. to go over the change," she said.

"Gag, that makes it sound like menopause," Max said. It came out quickly, and before he could feel regret for saying it, Layna smiled to let him know it was okay. That broke the ice, and everyone relaxed.

Then Crosby pushed again. A little too hard for Layna. “So, I guess you’ll need to select a piece to do?”

Nancy shook her head and pretended to be on a loudspeaker. “Inappropriate, party of one.” She glared at him.

Layna glared at Crosby. “Cros, not now.”

It was not the reaction he wanted, and Layna knew it. It was strange for her to feel she had rejected him when there was nothing to even reject. She thought he might have gone on to explain why his incredible writings and monologues would be perfect for her. Could make her shine. Make them *both* shine. But he stayed quiet, which was just fine with her.

For a short time there was awkward silence, save for Alice’s gum chewing. It gave Layna the opportunity to let Max know they were all right. She leaned her head on his shoulder. She may not have been happy, but she was sure the gesture worked wonders to make him happy.

It was short-lived. The doors to the room opened.

“Speaking of opportunity,” Nancy said. She motioned with her head and the group watched Dillon walk in. He had a guitar bag slung over his shoulder.

“Guess he didn’t get the memo on stalking,” Max said in a low voice.

Layna didn’t take the comment well and wondered how Max could have thought it would be taken otherwise. “He is not a stalker. Just give it a rest.”

“So defensive,” Alice uttered. “He may be weird, but at least he’s cute.”

She said it loud enough for Layna to know she wanted him to hear it. He did, and she watched him grin. It faded when his eyes met hers, and he gave her the look only she knew. It let her know he was there for her.

"And scene," Max said and stood up. He let his hand run down Layna's arm. She tried to grab it with hers, but he pulled it away.

Max kept his head down as he left and Layna noticed when he passed Dillon he purposely bumped him, just like the night in the theater. She watched as her ex-boyfriend's shoulder took the impact from her current boyfriend.

"Max?" Layna called out, both to get his attention and chastise him for yet another low blow.

Alice, Nancy, and Crosby looked at each other, the tension in the room rising.

"I think we're gonna head out, too," Nancy said, making it clear that whether they were done or not, they were done. The three of them stood up.

"Come by later, okay, Layn?" Alice said. "We'll, you know. I don't know." She shook her head as she left.

Nancy and Crosby followed, with Nancy turning back to Layna. She mouthed words that looked like *I'm sorry*. Layna grimaced as Nancy turned around.

Dillon stared down at Layna. "I sure know how to clear a room." He worked at a chuckle, but Layna gave him nothing. She couldn't even look at him. Instead she just wondered what he would say next. Another bad quip? Something about Max? Her friends? School? Sydney?

It didn't matter. Right then all she wanted to do, and all she did, was cry. Her shoulders jerked ever so slightly. And then she saw one of her tears hit the floor. She felt Dillon's hand on her shoulder. It was warm. Almost welcome. Then she jerked back immediately, instinctively. "No!"

Dillon pulled his hand back, and it looked to Layna like he did it in surrender. She stared at him and shook her head.

Tired, afraid, disgusted, she ran out of the cafeteria.

JINXED

Inside the school's security office, Daniel sat at his desk filling out paperwork. He never thought he had an easy job, but it wasn't difficult. Trask Academy of Performing Arts had a lot of rules in place for the students. And that meant a lot of kids would push boundaries to break them. Some of these rules, but not all, included the more obvious:

No smoking

No skipping class

Not being late to class

No exceptions to the dress code

And God forbid inappropriate physical contact between any students, no matter their sex.

Be it hair dyed an improper color, skirts too short, pants tapered at the bottom, or any other number of infractions, Daniel was sure he'd seen them all and knew that the kids definitely felt they were better than he was at being the fashion police.

The rule zealots, led by McKenna, made Daniel think back to his own high school experience. It was fraught with rules, too, but of the more incredible-to-believe kind. No hugging on campus—Catholic schools believed it led to teen pregnancy. No clothing with the number thirty-three on it—the city in which he grew up had a gang who called themselves the "33rd Street Cru." And, what might have been the most ludicrous of all, no hand-shaking amongst teams after any sporting event because it could lead to fights—an event that only happened twice out of hundreds of games, so the school's theory was spurious at best. The last rule would never play a part at Trask because they had no sporting teams. Extracurricular athletics, save for gymnastics and tumbling related to theatrics, were of little interest to most of the student body, or the board. So for his high school football fix Daniel would go to weekend games at Nardue Academy on the mainland.

As he finished his paperwork, Daniel made sure names were spelled right and transgressions correctly recorded. The newest issue on campus, though, was beyond him. For more than a few moments he had wondered if, at some point in the future, Trask would have to add a check box on student incident forms for death by suicide. The grim thought was fleeting, but it still floated in the recesses of his mind. He wished he could shake it off and leave it buried.

The door opened and Parker walked in.

Daniel stood to greet him. Parker nodded and gave a small grin.

“Anything I can do for you, detective?” Daniel asked.

“I’d like to make a couple calls, if that’s all right,” Parker answered without sarcasm. Daniel appreciated the straightforwardness. “I assume you have a landline here.”

“Sure. Yeah, of course.” Daniel shuffled files and papers out of the way so he could turn the phone toward Parker.

The detective went to sit down on the visitor chair in front of the metal desk. He had barely squatted when the door opened again.

It was McKenna.

The dean let the door close behind him, looking around as if he were surveying a room he had never been to.

“Dean, good evening, sir,” Daniel said, almost in reverence.

McKenna offered nothing back and it made the security officer think the man was a jerk. He knew McKenna was simply marking his territory. Then again, a student had been found dead.

The notion made Daniel feel a pang of selfish callousness.

Parker remained standing and turned to the dean. Daniel noticed the detective was just shy of a foot taller than the campus king. And the dean was not a short man. Daniel wondered how it must have made McKenna feel to have to look up to someone, literally.

"Dean, twice in one day. To what do we owe the pleasure?" Parker asked stiffly. Daniel could have bruised himself had he tried to run through the tension between the two men.

"May we speak in private?" McKenna said, not weakening his position by taking his eyes off Parker. Daniel hesitated, discerning McKenna's impolite way of telling him to leave. He put some paperwork in a neater pile, at which point McKenna cleared his throat. The security guard stopped arranging things on the desk, grabbed his walkie-talkie, and started for the door. As he stepped past McKenna, who was still staring at Parker, Daniel did not feel remorse when he thought, *It's your school, but my office, dickhead.*

With that, Daniel left.

"Looks like we're the main event," Parker said as he looked around the empty office. He watched McKenna, knowing full well the short, old man must have felt his domain was being invaded. It was then the dean spoke. Every word, Parker thought, sounded very well thought out. Maybe even rehearsed.

"Mr. Parker," the dean started, "I've been thinking about things since we last spoke, and let me be frank. Trask Academy of Performing Arts is not just a school for a child with a knack for dance. Or a child who can carry a tune. We have graduated some of the finest performing artists there are. And we have done it through the generous support of the alumni. I do not want to see that ruined by this terrible, isolated event."

By the time McKenna landed his last word he was standing directly opposite from Parker, and was now behind the desk. The detective almost grinned, thinking it was a clever strategy. He felt McKenna was more at ease with a barrier between them. But it also seemed clear the dean did it as a slight to remind Parker on whose property he stood.

Parker did not care and threw his adversary a steely gaze. "I apologize for not seeing it as clearly as you do." He stared down at the papers Daniel had tried to put together neatly. "You realize that this was not," he stopped for a second and grabbed one of the papers. Picking it up, he read, "*A student caught drinking at a school dance.*" His eyes glanced at another transgression. "*Or students caught getting too close behind the stage.*" He let the paper fall out of his hand, and it fluttered onto the floor. "One of your students did the unthinkable."

McKenna clenched his jaw. *Good*, Parker thought, knowing the dean had more than one goal in mind. The first was to be done with all of what he suggested was death nonsense. That bothered Parker. Death was never nonsense. The second was more practical, to stop mainlanders from snooping around any more than they needed to. If Parker didn't dislike the dean already, he might understand.

Then there was the third part.

"The unthinkable, yes," McKenna said, just as Parker knew he would. "Well, all the more reason to keep the story away from the eyes and ears of students, faculty, and, naturally, the press."

Parker cocked his head, and shook it the tiniest bit. "Why am I not surprised to hear your interest lies more with the welfare of the academy's coffers than with its students?"

"I think we are done here."

Parker watched him walk from behind the desk, past Parker, and toward the door to let himself out.

Parker raised his voice. It had an authoritative quality that almost made the dean stop. "A student in *your* charge is *dead*, yet you don't seem concerned. What makes you think it won't happen again?"

This time McKenna did stop. He turned toward Parker and spoke to him like a child.

"Because that girl can only kill herself once."

Parker watched McKenna slink out as the door closed behind him with a faint whoosh.

And he hated him for it.

Max sat on a stone alumni bench that had a sight line through a group of trees to the front gate. He had been irritable. With himself. With Layna. Or more specifically, Layna and Dillon.

He watched Daniel make his way along the gate. It looked to Max like he was mumbling. And he looked on edge. Max supposed that was to be expected. Weren't they all on edge? Taking care of minor student issues was a far cry from a student killing herself. And this wasn't just any student, he reminded himself. This was Sydney Miller. He fought back the urge to stand up and ask how much Daniel was making for being a glorified babysitter, and then, whatever the number, to say it wasn't enough.

Instead Max sat quietly. He wasn't trying to hide from Daniel, but he didn't do anything to make himself known, either. He just watched as Daniel moved to the massive front gates of the campus and handled the nightly ritual called Gate Lock. With everything going on, Max felt, for maybe just the first time, that they were in something more akin to a low-security prison than an elite prep school. The food was certainly not much better, at least from what he saw on MSNBC's *Lock Up*. And he was stuck with people he didn't always like.

Daniel opened the electronic security box to the left of the entrance, and Max watched as the wrought iron monstrosity closed, bringing together two letters that signified the school's name. T for Trask and A for Academy. When they clanked together Max thought what all the young men thought, *Trapped again in T and* A.

As Daniel walked away, still grumbling about whatever it he was grumbling about, Max eyed him conspiratorially, wondering what those thoughts might be. Then his own mind turned back to Layna. And tits and ass.

He and Layna hadn't gone too far. Max knew Layna was a good girl. He chided himself when he wondered how good a girl she was when she was dating Dillon. He shook off the thought. Not much seemed to happen between them and, in fact, Max remembered hearing the swirling rumor Dillon might even be gay.

"Are you done being mad at me?" Layna's voice said.

The surprise arrival made Max jump, even as she rested a hand on his shoulder. He didn't turn around. He was also glad Layna was not a mind reader.

"Watching Gate Lock isn't quite the sunset, but being closed off seems kind of fitting right now, don't you think?" He still wasn't looking at her as he felt her arm drape around his shoulder.

Layna sat down next to him. "Listen, Dillon and I—"

"Dillon and you, what?" Max asked, staring forward. He wanted to stay angry. Stoic. Something.

"I'm with you. Only you," she said.

Max felt a tickle of loose threads on his hand from a bracelet Layna wore, something Nancy had given her. She tried to interlock her fingers into his, but he didn't budge. Then he budged a little. "Why won't he just go away?"

"Because we're still friends," Layna answered sweetly, honestly. "And where exactly do you want him to go?"

Max finally turned to her, his head moving in a way that suggested she would not want him to answer that question.

"There's friends, and then there's you and Dillon. He finds a way to be near you. *All* the time."

"You're exaggerating."

"Am I?" Max knew he was right. He could see Layna thinking on that. He also knew that while she didn't put things into any kind of Dillon-Layna proximity coefficient formula or anything, she had to see it.

"Layn, everyone notices," he continued. "That's why they always get nervous when El Strange-o turns up."

Layna pulled her hand back from his and crossed her arms. A small smile grew on her face as she turned to him.

"Wait a minute. They, or you?" she asked. "Um, are you jealous?"

Max grinned. "You'd like that, wouldn't you? But, sorry, I am so not jealous."

"Then prove it and hold my hand, would you?" she said more than asked.

Max obliged, taking her hand into his. The touch instantly put him at ease. He pulled her close to him and gave her a kiss.

They stood up together and started toward the dorms in silence, their arms swinging in unison with every step.

"And, by the way, he's quiet, not strange," Layna said.

Max laughed. "Wow, you made it a full, what, five seconds. Was that defense just bubbling up inside you?"

"No. I don't know. Maybe a little," Layna admitted. "But if it makes you feel better, I'll be staying the night with you. Not him."

This stopped Max dead. For the smallest of moments, his maleness hoped his good girl was about to go bad. "Really?" he asked in a way that oozed romantic potential.

"Get your mind out of the gutter. I just don't wanna be alone," Layna said. "We are stranded together on an island, after all."

"Oh, so now you're stranded with me?" Max wondered playfully.

Layna nuzzled her head onto his shoulder. "Yes, definitely. But it's good. And tonight I want it to be just us."

Max felt a slight pressure building. Hormones pulsing. "Sounds dangerous."

"Easy, cowboy."

Max stopped and turned her to him. Gently, he placed a hand under her chin. She smiled sweetly, which gave way to the deep kiss that followed. Max felt her give in as she wrapped her arms around him.

He looked down at her, kissed her forehead, and then focused intently on Layna. On the moment. He was completely unaware that somebody, far closer to them than he could even imagine, was watching.

Alice gnawed her gum, blowing bubble after bubble as she sat in the center of the cold, metal risers in the black box theater. She was there to critique Crosby and Nancy as they rehearsed yet another of Crosby's illusions.

The gum-chomping slowed as she thought about why Crosby wasted so much time trying to master the art of deception. It wasn't that he wasn't good, though he wasn't great, if she were to be honest. It just seemed so futile. She had been to Las Vegas. She felt magicians with any modicum of merit always went there to perform, but also stayed there, moving from big resort to smaller hotel to the old strip, and then *poof!* They disappeared like their best worst tricks. She remembered two things about Sin City: it was hotter and drier than she imagined any place with living people should be and, potentially more frightening, the huge billboards of magician Lance Burton that seemed to be everywhere. She giggled at the memory of their tagline, "You will always remember …" and his gigantic face, painted in a way that made him seem like a ventriloquist doll. And not in a *Happy go lucky look how funny my dummy* is way, but more like a *Wow, he's had a lot of plastic surgery for a man, Joan Rivers would have been proud* way. Alice and the other girl her age, the daughter of her parents' friends whose name she couldn't remember, kept telling her she thought she was talented enough to go to a special school, used to joke that it wasn't that they'd "always remember," but that the obscene number of billboards simply wouldn't allowed them to forget. Alice wasn't sure what happened to the girl. It was the first time in a long time she thought about what's-her-face.

Alice revisited in her mind the long talks she and Crosby had, late at night when he snuck into her room, usually after he and Nancy had a fight. He talked about how badly he wanted to be a playwright. She talked about how badly she wanted to be the next Oprah. Or the next Ellen, since Oprah was off the air, but she was still, you know, *Oprah*. She would joke that she didn't want to be Ellen in the lesbian way. She was never sure if Crosby found that funny.

She never told Crosby, in those late night talks, how much she envied Nancy for dating him. She and Crosby sat so close, and spoke so candidly, that she had to stop herself more than once from leaning in with the hope that he might kiss her.

All the past, Alice thought, watching him and Nancy.

The two worked on an illusion. Crosby would be placed in a small trunk and then, he hoped, disappear. They shifted effortlessly around the stage, and each other, to music by Lady Gaga that was good but didn't quite seem to fit the situation. Alice envied Nancy in her sequined outfit, a little too tight and a little too revealing, with high heels a little too high for Alice's taste. *Bitch can work those stilettos.* Crosby looked equally dapper and dorky in a faux tuxedo, red-lined black cape, and top hat. Alice wasn't sure whether she liked the retro kitsch or just thought it was all too kitsch.

Alice had to admit that they were a fun duo to watch. Nancy, the shimmering sex goddess, helped Crosby, the goofy and lovable lead man, into the trunk. As he squeezed himself in, he lowered his hand dramatically, and Alice simultaneously thought that if he pulled the trick off, it would be amazing, and that there was no way he would pull it off.

Once Crosby was inside the impossibly small box, Nancy closed the top and locked it. She strutted her stuff, threw in a high kick for good measure, and let an opaque sheet flutter down to cover the top of the trunk completely. The music crescendoed as Nancy did an exaggerated hand gesture and a few quick twirls. Alice found it silly, designed to distract the audience from whatever Crosby was doing under the sheet and inside the trunk. Still, she thought, *If I were a lesbian, this would be working.*

Nancy glided over in time with the beat, pulled the sheet away, and looked disappointed.

The trunk was still there. Locked.

Alice leaned forward, wondering if there was more. Was this part of the trick?

Nancy stopped slithering and went to the CD player. She hit stop, and the black box theater seemed eerily quiet as Alice, a bubble deflating on her face, awaited Crosby's fate.

Alice jerked back in her seat at a pounding noise that came from the trunk. Nancy looked nonplussed as she yanked open the trunk, allowing Crosby to literally spill out as the box tipped over.

Alice clapped with a decided hesitancy, but she stopped when her two friends glared at her. Apparently, mission critical had failed. But she still thought Crosby looked cute.

Alice followed Nancy and Crosby outside, and the three of them walked from the theater across campus.

"I told you, I'll get it," Crosby insisted. "If my life depends on it, I'll nail the trick, all right?"

"Don't bite my head off," Nancy said, glaring. "It's not like you even have to get it."

Alice knew that one would sting. The tiny pang of hope that maybe, just maybe, there was going to be a rift between the two ended fast as he laughed.

"Sorry," he said to Nancy. He scratched at his head through a mane of hair. "I'm just pissed it's not working. And then this whole *Not now, Crosby* thing with Layna. I'm pissed and distracted. I just want my shot, you know."

Alice jumped in. "No kidding, but are we surprised? Layna talked enough about wanting Syd's position, then she gets it. Why can't you? It's all so weird."

"Nice, Alice. The whole empathy thing is really working out well for you." Nancy gave her a look Alice summed up as bitch at best.

"I'm just saying," Alice snapped, quietly popping her gum. Nancy squinted at the sound Alice knew she hated.

"Gum is gonna kill you, just watch," Nancy said. "And don't make me tweet at Cher about it. You love her and she hates gum."

"Like you know," Alice said.

"Fine, whatevs, but I know you love her and she does not love gum."

Crosby shook his head. "Can we not dwell on Cher, or gum, or Syd's untimely death? It's sad, all of it, and not something I really wanna keep thinking about."

There was little else to say, so he stopped talking. Alice looked from the ground to her friends, then back to the ground. "Does she really hate gum?"

Nancy snorted.

"Do you think Layna got my email?" Crosby asked as he nervously rolled a coin between his fingers. It shattered the illusion that he was trying to stay off the subject of Sydney's suicide.

"Which one of the way, way, way too many emails bugging my girlfriend after everything that's happened are you talking about?" Max said, coming up from behind them. His sudden appearance scared Alice.

"Where'd you come from?" Crosby asked.

Max punched Crosby in the arm, then put his arms around the ladies.

"Ow, you douche," Crosby yelped. "What are you doing sneaking around behind us?"

"Do I look like a sneaker?" Max answered. "I was with the woman of the hour."

"How is she?" Nancy asked.

Alice added, "We haven't really seen her since she … left."

Alice looked at Nancy for support, knowing there was really no other way to explain the last time they saw her.

"Better," Max shrugged. "She's having her tête-à-tête with McKenna and Mrs. D. now."

"Well, I didn't know what she'd want to tackle for the showcase, so I sent her a bunch of my stuff," Crosby said.

This time Alice was the one who looked at him as if he hadn't been paying any attention to what was going on. "No pressure," she offered sarcastically.

Max shook his head. "Did you just lose time? Reality check. Stop mulling over how to get in to Layna's head with your quest for fame."

No one noticed that the coin stopped flipping in Crosby's fingers. It landed in his palm where he grasped it tightly. So tightly his knuckles went white. He stared intently ahead, looking past Max. Past Nancy. And past Alice.

"She got her big break, what else does she want?" Crosby asked.

Max put his arm out to stop Crosby. "Dude!"

Crosby closed his eyes and put his head down. "I just meant—"

Max let his arm drop. Alice and Nancy marveled at the confrontation.

"I'm sure you're at the top of her list, but you need to lay off it," Max said with a finality.

Alice knew Max. He meant it.

"Fine, whatever, you're right. I get it." Crosby took a hesitant step forward, then stopped. He didn't look back at any of his friends. "Listen, I need to practice. Disappearing through a trap door is harder than it sounds." He turned to Nancy. "And, hey, you never know when you'll need to do it."

Nancy shrugged at Max and Alice and skipped toward Crosby. "Right behind you."

Alice was simultaneously elated and concerned when she watched Crosby wriggle, annoyed, away from Nancy's touch.

"Cros, come on," Nancy said.

He finally looked Nancy in the eyes. It was without warmth, without feeling. "I didn't say we."

With a shake of his head, he stepped away and was gone. Nancy wanted to follow, but Max stopped her. "Let him go."

"What's up with him?" Alice asked.

Nancy scoffed and Alice glared at her, sending a *This is not my fault* look.

"You know what, forget it," Nancy said in a softened tone. "Maybe he's got the right idea. Look out for number one, you know. Especially at this place. Ta-ta." Without hugging anyone, she walked away.

Alice watched her friend's sequins sparkle. She called out, "I'm sorry!"

Nancy didn't turn back, but she raised a hand in acceptance.

"And be careful!" Max said.

Nancy slowed, turned around to face them, and stepped slowly backward. "What? You think I'm gonna pull a Sydney?"

Alice looked at Max and wondered whether he felt the same way she did. Perhaps she even hoped. And for the first time, and for the smallest of moments, she was afraid of what was happening to her circle of friends.

Walls of dark wood surrounded Layna. She stared at diplomas, photos, accolades, and all of the other accoutrements placed to make sure anyone visiting the office knew the dean was important. Or rich. Or powerful.

Layna sat silently in the office of the very important, rich, and powerful Dean McKenna. She stopped looking around the room and recognized her two choices were to stare the administrator in the eye or look down at his desk, which he sat behind. She chose the latter. It was made of rich mahogany. She thought it was an antique. Then thought how gauche McKenna was.

Seated next to her was D'Arcangelo, and Layna could sense the woman's feelings were completely at odds with the dean's. It made her wonder how the two had worked together so well, and for so long. Apparently opposites do attract.

McKenna was droning on as D'Arcangelo kept a watchful, motherly regard on Layna. The young girl looked around the desk, first at the expensive pens, glass paperweights, and other inconsequential items that looked untouched. Then her eyes found something she could not ignore.

The photos of Sydney's room. Layna could only make out bits and pieces. The slight shambles the place appeared to be in. An open window. An umbrella.

An open umbrella.

Weird, Layna thought.

McKenna continued to speak, but Layna was only half-listening. Something about opportunity, something about chance. His hands brushed over the photos, careless as to whether he touched them. The dean's cufflink caught the edge of a photo, sliding it ever so slightly, revealing another photo underneath it.

Blood.

Layna's insides flopped when she saw Sydney's twisted arm, wrapped around her own body in an impossible manner. The girl's blonde hair tinged red. The dean tried to cover the offending images without appearing to do so.

Layna noticed his unease. She looked up at McKenna.

"What I meant is that time stands still for no one," McKenna said. "Not even now. This is an important moment for you, young lady, having secured one of the very limited slots in the showcase." He clasped his hands together righteously, as if he had just delivered a rousing sermon.

"I understand," Layna answered quietly. "What you're saying. I just don't know if I can do it. If I'm ready." If she could have wished it all away, wished herself far away, back to her grandparents' house, she would have.

McKenna blanched. "Participation in the showcase has always been coveted. There are plenty of other seniors who would gladly take your place. Think of how proud your mother would be."

Layna's face scrunched. She stared at him, disgusted that the dean had not only thrown some kind of ultimatum at her, but that he dared to bring her mother into the conversation. "How dare you." The words came out quiet, but full of malice. "I don't need you pretending to know anything she would ever think."

D'Arcangelo placed her hand on Layna's shoulder. "Layna's going to be fine," she said, and Layna felt a light squeeze. "She's strong. Stronger than she knows."

"I guess I don't know what to say right now." Layna sighed.

"Say you are thrilled. What girl wouldn't be?" McKenna asked with rhetorical incredulity.

Layna looked at him sharply and delivered a response like a dart. "Sydney." She wanted to call him an asshole, which he was, but she bit her tongue and scraped her chair back on the floor.

She stood, defiant. "Are we done?"

D'Arcangelo nodded, motioning to the dean that it was time to let this rest. For now.

Layna started toward the door.

"I was talking about the opportunity, not the circumstance," McKenna specified.

Layna's head dropped as she shook it. *I can't believe him*, she thought, then she turned to the right, just enough so that he could see her speak but she wouldn't have to look at him. "To some, they're one in the same. And don't you ever, ever, talk about my mother again. You didn't know her. And you clearly don't know me."

D'Arcangelo watched her exit, then turned to the dean.

He cleared his throat, seemingly unfazed. "All things considered, I would say that went better than expected."

D'Arcangelo appeared uneasy. None of this was sitting well with her. She stared down at McKenna. "I wouldn't say that at all."

Outside of McKenna's office, Layna leaned against a grand trophy case. Her reflection watched her as she stared forward.

D'Arcangelo made her way over, just as Layna expected she would. The teacher was silent as she moved a stray piece of hair from the girl's face.

"Should I really be doing this?" Layna asked, shrugging as she wiped away tears with one hand.

"Let me ask you this," D'Arcangelo said, "and please know I am coming from a very, very different place than the dean: why *shouldn't* you do it?"

"People expected to see Sydney. Now she's gone. She's dead." Layna finally looking at her teacher. "I'm left to deal with it, to deal with my friends. I have to pick my own play, a cast, crew. Mrs. D., I'm stuck between choosing my friends for the wrong reasons and having them angry at me for the right ones."

D'Arcangelo nodded, and Layna felt that the woman understood. That, or she was a better actress than anyone knew. "Ah, they're gunning for their moment."

"I guess," Layna shrugged again.

"I can only tell you, regardless of the why, this is now your moment," D'Arcangelo stated with sincerity. "Your opportunity to shine. And if you take it, and I think you should, choose something with meaning. A piece which speaks to you. That means something."

D'Arcangelo stepped in front of Layna and brought the girl's face to her own with a hand under her chin. Nothing at this moment felt to Layna like it was wrong, or fabricated, or full of hidden meaning. Layna wanted to do it, she felt she had earned it, even if feeling that came with a pang of guilt.

"You can do this," the older woman said. "For yourself and, yes, even for Sydney. We don't know what was going on in her mind, but I do believe she would be proud of you."

D'Arcangelo let go of Layna's soft face and marched down the hallway, receding to nothing more than a silhouette in the harsh light and a blurry reflection in the polished wooden floor.

CHAPTER V

The main library of the campus was a two-story stone and marble monster which did not speak softly about the copious donations it took to build. There were other buildings on the campus that housed books and resources but were relegated to areas designated by major, either dance, music, theater, or telecommunications.

Inside this building, though, were the school's main assets. And they were plenty. The structure comprised bookshelves, mazes of hallways, and meeting rooms in a space so big, most wondered if it would look full even if every student and teacher entered at once.

Nothing could be too subtle at Trask.

In one of the research rooms, tall stacks of books, antique furniture that looked expensive and uncomfortable, and garish lighting some architect had deemed gorgeous, completed the picture.

Layna sat at one of the few tables, situated amongst boxes, books, and papers stacked high. She read, and every so often, she pushed the waft of hair that dangled into her view back behind her ear, where it didn't seem to want to stay.

But she wasn't alone. Max was close, with manuscripts piled in his strong arms, and Alice, who looked through the nearby computer catalog.

Max dumped the contents from his bundle onto the table as Layna looked up at him, exasperated. She shoved the material from in front of her, put her head down, and pretended to bang it.

"You chose to do this," Max said.

Alice shook her head, still staring at the bluish computer screen.

"Yeah, well, I did not choose wisely. I don't think I can do *this*," Layna offered, gesturing to the ludicrous amount of material surrounding her on the table, "anymore."

"But the night is still young," Max whispered. He nibbled on Layna's ear as she giggled and pulled away. "Okay, I have an idea. Let's take a break, get some food, and come back to this later."

"Done," Layna said immediately. She stood up, stretched, grabbed her bag, and then looked at Alice. The girl was still buried in whatever was on the screen in front of her.

"Hey, Diane Sawyer, the train is heading out," Max said.

Alice did not stop reading to look at him. "One more minute."

"Which will turn into forever," Layna added.

"The computer will still be there, I promise," Max said. "C'mon, let's grab grub. I have a vision of overpriced and under-flavored pre-packaged sandwiches calling out to be eaten." He laughed.

Alice hit a few keys, then swiveled toward them in her chair. "Go on without me. I'm not starving and, seriously, you guys are probably desperate for a little time without a third wheel."

"Alice, stop," Layna said softly. She liked how sincere and earnest Alice was.

"Nice, no third wheel. Ready for a ride on my motorcycle," Max said. He grabbed Layna and growled playfully.

"Ew, dear God help us all. Alice, you cannot leave me alone with this lunatic," Layna pleaded.

Max stepped back and pretended to be offended. "Ew? Moi?"

Layna raised an eyebrow and hoped he got the message. *Yes, sir.*

Alice laughed. "Seriously. Go. Have fun. Besides, I think I'm on to finding the secrets NBC didn't want anyone to know about the whole Matt Lauer slash Ann Curry debacle."

Layna cleared her throat.

"*After* I find your perfect piece of material, of course," Alice said. Layna was not at all convinced.

"Has anyone ever pointed out your slight obsession with the Today Show?" Max asked.

"So false," Alice said seriously. "I'm totally obsessed with *Matt Lauer.*"

Layna didn't get it at all. An older, balding co-anchor of a morning news infotainment show wasn't who most people expected a high school senior, even one interested in a career in solid television journalism, to be watching. Much less watching fanatically.

"You guys have never Googled shirtless Matt Lauer, obvi," Alice said, as if reading Layla's mind.

Max put his hand to his chest, throwing an effeminate cadence into his voice. "Well, obvi totes hilar, I mean, like, really. Matt Lauer, *dreamboat.*"

Layna laughed and elbowed him in the stomach. "That's our cue. We'll be back."

Max offered his arm to Layna, and she wrapped hers around it. As they moved, Layna's attention was snagged by something on the screen in front of Alice. She yanked Max to check out the image of a very well-toned Matt Lauer running on the beach, sans shirt, sporting a six pack.

"What up?" Max asked.

Layna raised her eyebrows at Alice, then turned to Max. "Oh, totes nothing."

Layna winked at Alice and laughed as she and Max walked away. For some reason, and she couldn't say what or why, a pang of unease fell upon her at leaving Alice all alone.

She'll be fine, a more reasonable voice inside Layna thought as the heavy front doors shut behind her and Max.

The two hopped down the library steps. Then Layna ran from Max as he playfully chased and tried to tickle her. She broke away, then turned to face him, moving backward.

Right into Dillon.

Her laughter turned into a short scream. She covered her mouth and turned around to see her former boyfriend.

"You scared me," Layna admitted, backing away from him and moving closer to Max.

"Sorry." He looked at Layna, then to Max, who made him nervous. "I was just—I mean, I wanted—"

Max stepped forward, accusingly. "Just what? Wanted to what, man?"

It almost appeared to Dillon that Max made himself look bigger, as if he were some sort of animal protecting its prize. It didn't sit well with him, and he let Layna know with a look.

"Max, come on. Stop," she told him.

Dillon was relieved as Max took a heavy, deep breath and turned away.

"I'm really trying here," Max admitted, "but this is what I was talking about. His creeping around you."

"I go to school here, too," Dillon declared, annoyed. He knew he might not be able to take Max in a physical fight, but he was getting tired of all of this, too. "And, by the way, it's the *library*. You don't have a corner on the market, you know."

"Thanks for the update, dickweed. And here's one for you.

The music building, where you work on all your pseudo-cool emo crap, is on the other side of campus, with its own library for your pussy needs. Yet you always seem to wander over to wherever Layna is."

Layna stepped in front of a heated, pacing Max. "Enough!" She looked at her boyfriend and mouthed *stop*. Her eyes pleaded, but Max wasn't done.

He nudged past Layna and stepped right to Dillon, forcing the point that he was taller, bigger, and stronger.

"Listen, bud, you and Layna? That song is played out," Max sneered. "She's with me now, so if you're smart, you'll just slang dip."

Dillon held his ground. "This is ridiculous," he said. "She and I are friends."

Max turned to Layna. "Aww, you're still friends. How sweet." He turned back to Dillon, who could feel Max look at him with pity. "And that's all you're ever gonna be, you freaked out loser!"

Max shoved Dillon, hard. Dillon lost his footing and stumbled back, embarrassed.

"Max!" squealed Layna.

"Watch it, Layna, looks like your boyfriend here has some anger issues," Dillon said. Then he added pointedly, "You never know what he's capable of."

"What the hell does that mean?" Max asked, more heated.

"You tell me, tough guy," Dillon retorted. He knew it wasn't a good idea to test Max's limits, but the adrenaline coursing through him spoke hastily.

The two were ready to come to blows, until Layna pushed past them. "Forget it! Beat the crap out of each other for all I care!"

Max called after her as she stormed away. "Where are you going?"

She did not turn around, but the anger in her voice came

through, pelting both Dillon and Max. "To find Crosby and Nan. To be anywhere but where you are now," she said.

As Max watched Layna disappear into the early evening, Dillon snickered. Max shot him a look.

"Sounds like you really have your finger on the pulse of what she wants," Dillon taunted, again second-guessing why he might be starting something dangerous.

"Screw. You!" Max wound his arm back and balled his hand into a fist, ready for the punch. Until his hand was grabbed from behind. Max turned around.

It was McKenna. Dillon was surprised at the strength the dean seemed to have and looked on as Max pulled his fist away with some effort as he tried to compose himself.

McKenna rubbed his fingers, as if touching Max was something dirty. "Mister Reynolds. At it again? What do you say we calm down and head over to my office?"

"But, he—"

McKenna waved a hand and pointed for Max to proceed.

Dillon smirked at Max and knew he had won, at least for now.

The dean forced Max on his way but shot a look to Dillon. "We'll deal with you another time. For now, I suggest you find a constructive way to occupy yourself."

As he and Max walked away, Dillon could hear their conversation as it faded.

"You knew Sydney Miller," the dean said. "Someone wants to speak with you."

The voice trailed off, and Dillon could only see their mouths moving, then nothing. He smiled, pleased with himself.

He turned and stared at the library.

CHAPTER VI

Alice's gum bubble burst. She worked her tongue, now blue with the color of the sugary, berry-flavored treat, around her lips to bring it back into her mouth. She was still seated in front of the computer, her mouth agape as she stared at the screen. Something had not simply caught her attention, but yanked at her as she made sense of what she'd uncovered.

"Amazeballs," she said quietly, as if she didn't want to reveal a secret, then went back to chewing. She furiously clicked and scrolled, shaking her head as her eyes scanned back and forth. With a few keystrokes, she printed the documents and rose from her seat to grab them from the printer but stopped when a loud noise echoed from outside the research room. Startled, she turned around but saw nothing. She looked over at the printer display. It blinked *Warming Up*, so she moved her gaze to the entryway and leaned down to grab her bag. When the printer started to make a churning sound, she turned back to it.

But there were still no pages. *Calibrating.*

"Jesus," she huffed.

There was little time to be annoyed when Alice heard another noise. Another too loud noise. And it was closer to her. She slung her backpack over her shoulder, looked at the printer, and then the door. She had a decision to make, and she decided it was time to leave.

After exiting the research room slowly, she walked to the edge of the balcony. It overlooked an expansive area with a half winding staircase on each side. Looking down at the floor made it easier to see the two designs in the marble, outlined by thin lines of golden metal. Although they were not elaborately detailed, they looked like the interconnecting symbols of a square and a ruler. Alice knew what it meant.

The symbol of the Freemasons.

She had heard the stories and knew they were never officially confirmed nor denied by anyone affiliated with the school. But most people assumed that's what they were meant to represent. Most of the students understood the Masons were said to have marginalized women. Or were a secret society many churches condemned. Or something very History Channel like that. It all seemed like nonsense to Alice, though it made her think of something she hadn't thought of before. That the whole idea could make a great investigative story. She'd just have to convince her moderator, the AV Club and, most unlikely of all, McKenna.

Another sound broke her from her rambled thoughts. Her gum-chewing stopped. This time the noise sounded like the thud of heavy books on the marble floor. It was closer than the others. Somewhere below her.

But closer, Alice thought. Definitely closer. Her voice was quiet, though she tried to project confidence as she called out. "Layna? Max? You guys back already?"

There was no sound in return. She crept forward to the edge of the balcony, carefully leaned over the smooth steel railing, and craned her head in the hope that she might see something. Or somebody.

"Hello?" she called out again, this time with less coolness. A shadow glided across the floor below her.

"Oh my God!" Alice screamed. As she jerked back, she couldn't stop her book bag from sliding off her shoulder, down her arm, over the railing, and onto the shiny floor below. It landed with a crumple, followed by a tiny jingle when her keys slid out from the front pocket. They lay next to the bag, still connected to the white cat keychain, the smiling puss of the pussy staring up at her.

"Dammit!" Alice whispered, staring down. There was no more shadow, no more sound. But she didn't imagine it. Him. Them. Whatever.

Running her hand along the cold, metal railing, Alice made her way along the balcony to the staircase. She descended with purpose at first, but began to slow almost as if by instinct. Each step resonated with an echoed click when her short heels made contact with the cold, hard stairs.

She reached the first level and looked around before taking the final steps to her book bag. She zipped up the front pocket and pulled it toward her. Her keychain was no longer there. *No, no, no*, she thought with a tinge of fear.

She didn't have time to dwell on the creeping horror that her keys were gone. That they might have been taken. She heard a soft click and looked down the long hallway behind her to see the lights going off, one row at a time, as if it were part of some game. Toying with her. Scaring her.

Then she saw something on the floor. A glint. Her keychain. The metal carabiner that linked the keys to the fluffy, white cat reflected the light above her that had yet to be extinguished.

Alice understood that she didn't have much time as the darkness that consumed the building got closer.

"Stop turning off the lights!" Alice yelled to the doors, to the person she didn't see but knew must be there. She hoped it was Daniel, or someone she knew.

The lights continued to go out. Alice felt a physical weight press upon her at the thought that her keys were so far from her, now in a sea of darkness.

They were also near the exit. She felt like a child again, when she was afraid to stay at her grandparents' house. It was there her grandfather, the father of her mother, had threatened to put her in the basement if she was a bad girl. It only took one time for him to show her how the darkness crept up the stairs from the damp, dirt floor for her to be silent, and good, each time. It seemed even now that she could smell the musty air of Pawpaw's basement.

The light above her went off. Everything was cloaked in darkness, save for the pale shafts of moonlight that fell in from the skylights above.

"Damn," Alice mumbled. She grabbed her bag, opened it, and shoved her hand around the contents. She pulled out a mini flashlight and turned it on. Its small halo of light was barely enough to illuminate more than a few feet in front of her, but it was all she had. She took her first hesitant step forward, only to be stopped by a sudden flash of lightning. It was followed by a crackle of thunder that simmered before exploding into a boom that she felt.

Alice looked up. She couldn't see the first drops of rain, but she could hear the noise they made when they hit the glass high above her.

The darkness and the coming storm coalesced into something which found its way under Alice's skin. She was upset, she was scared. But she needed to get her keys and get out of there.

Through the intermittent thunder and lightning, Alice stepped forward, guided by the glow of her flashlight. She focused on the bright red letters of the exit sign ahead of her. She looked to her left. The darkness overcame even the bookcases that were only a few feet away. It made her wonder what might be hiding. What waited to get her.

Alice shook her head. "Get a grip." But she hated having to do this. Of course, there was nothing behind her, nothing around her. But at the same time, she could be wrong.

A burst of air hit her from behind. Something rushed past her.

"Who's there? Who is *that*?" She scanned the area with her flashlight.

There was no reply but thunder. Alice turned back, accelerated her pace, and ran to her goal, the keys ahead. Finally, she made it. She bent down to pick them up and saw the cat was no longer on them. She manipulated the keychain and keys around in her hand as if she could somehow find the white fluff of the cat. It was futile. The cat was gone. It had been torn off.

Alice had had enough. She ran to the exit and yanked on the doors. But they were locked. She pulled on them, harder. They would not give.

"No!" she yelled as panic rose within her. She stepped to the thin window next to the door and pressed her face against it. She could barely see anything through the antique, bubbled glass and the streaks of rain that came down harder and harder.

"Damn." She looked at the keys in her hand, then back to the hallways she had traversed in the dark. She turned toward the door again and tried to see out the window. A flash of lightning illuminated the outside, but there was no one to be seen.

When the lightning faded, and the thunder stopped its song, she backed an inch away from the glass and stared at her own reflection.

And that was when she saw the distorted, twisted mask of the killer pop up behind her.

Alice screamed, turned, and ducked as the knife in the killer's hand lunged for her throat. The blade flashed an electric blue as lightning colored the sky.

The attacker's violent momentum sent him stumbling toward the door, and Alice used his split-second faltering to tear down the hallway. The darkness in front of her seemed like no worry in the world compared to the darkness from which she ran. Her heart felt thick and tired as she ran and screamed, "Help me! Someone please help me!" Her legs strained and her lungs burned. She panted when she reached the end of the hallway, which left her only one way to go.

Up.

She pivoted on the supposed Freemason symbology under her feet and ran back toward the second-floor staircase, pushing her body into overdrive. If she didn't, the killer would meet her at the bottom of the stairs.

But as she leapt to grasp the railing, the killer caught up to her and his knife connected with her forearm in a deep slash. She yelped in pain as a line of blood formed in the gash. Still, she moved forward, she had to, and pulled herself up the stairs. This time she made the mistake of looking back, losing her balance as the killer approached just a few steps behind. She stumbled, and her face slammed down against the marble stairs. Everything seemed to stop. Then she screamed as blood and front teeth ejected from her mouth.

The world around Alice came back with pain as the blade sank deep into her calf. She screamed, cried. It was more pain than she could imagine, but she turned her body around when the knife pulled out. The killer raised it high above, ready for the final strike, but Alice kicked him with every ounce of her being. Her eyes went wide when she saw it worked. The blow forced the attacker back, and he tumbled down the stairs.

Alice tried to regain her thoughts and knew there was no time to savor the small victory. She hobbled to her feet, fought through the pain, and ran up the stairs to disappear inside the blackness of the research room. She looked behind her, worried there would be blood trailing behind her on the floor, an absolute giveaway. She was relieved to see that there wasn't. Instead she saw the sticky, thick red travel down her leg, past her knife-slashed jeans, and pool at her bright yellow socks.

Alice slinked into the tall book stacks that filled the room like a maze. Sweat beaded on her upper lip and snot dripped from her nose as she peered through shelved tomes that provided cover. She did not have to look for long. The masked killer had entered the room. He was illuminated by the computer monitor, the only light other than intermittent flashes of lightning.

Alice sucked in shallow, quiet breaths. She watched as the man went to the computer and yanked its cord out of the socket. With a spark, the computer went dead. She could barely see the person in black, but cringed when she heard the knife being raked along the shelves. The soft clink it made as it dragged from book spine to book spine let Alice know where the attacker was.

The attacker got closer and closer. Alice quietly turned a corner as the killer slinked to the aisle she had just vacated. It was a game of cat and mouse, and Alice stayed one small step ahead. She rounded a bookcase, then the killer did. She snuck down an aisle, then shifted, and the killer did the same.

Then he stopped.

Alice stayed rigid and made sure she could see where the killer was. She barely held her breath as the man with the knife got closer. And closer. She felt she was safe, until she dropped her mini flashlight. She covered her mouth in horror as it rolled on the ground to the end of the aisle, flickering, dimming.

Alice watched with terror as the killer moved with insane purpose, no fear, no question, knife ready. Reaching the flashlight, he bent down to pick it up and turned the corner.

But Alice was not there. She watched as he looked around, confused at seeing only a cubby of shelves. No exit. No way out. Alice knew the time had come. She stared at the killer as he turned his head upward, fast, eyeing the one place he had not looked for her.

Alice made eye contact and screamed from above, where she had hidden on the top of a shelf she had climbed. She haphazardly pushed books, magazines, and boxes down on the killer. She smiled as they hit him, and she could see he was dazed. He flailed his arms, as Alice continued the barrage until there was nothing left to heave over the edge.

Alice saw her chance and leapt down beside the confused killer. The silver blade sliced outward, but she jumped back fast enough to avoid it. She grabbed the killer's arm and rammed it into the edge of a shelf. The impact forced the knife to drop to the floor.

Alice took off. She had the lead, had more time. She was just about out of the room when she turned and saw the killer staring at her, ready with another trick.

The killer grabbed book after book and slid them hard across the floor, faster than Alice's chunky legs could carry her. She was just at the exit when one of the books found its target and tripped her up. She stumbled forward and caught herself on the railing of the balcony. The killer ran toward her with an angry purpose. Alice threw her arms up to protect her face from the heavy books being hurled at her.

Alice screamed when a book connected with her right cheek, the corner digging in just below her eye. It threw her off balance, and she toppled halfway over the railing. She held tight with one hand and tried not to fall. The other hand clutched at her throat as her body sent mixed signals about what to do.

For a split second Alice did not know what was going on, and then the gum in her mouth found its way into her throat. She choked on it.

Alice was frantically trying to breathe, trying to cry, trying to live. She saw the long way down below her. When she looked back up, a scream welled inside her but could not come out.

The killer stood right above her.

Alice gasped for air. Tears filled in her eyes. She shook her head back and forth in place of screaming. *Please, God, no*, she thought.

The killer stared down at her, and Alice watched in horror as he nodded. She felt a searing pain as the blade, timed with a bolt of lightning outside, raked across her fingers and sliced them clean off.

Blood spurted in four arcs where her digits once were, and Alice fell through the darkness. The last thing she saw was the blue hue of lightning as it colored the mask her killer wore, then her body hit the floor with a sickening, wet crunch. The gum in her throat dislodged as if from a deadly Heimlich maneuver. It landed next to her turned head and dead, open eyes with a dull plop.

CHAPTER VII

Layna soaked up thick drops of rain in what had become a torrential downpour. It was a futile effort, but she held a hand over her head like it might provide shelter as she ran toward the dance studio.

She was still mad at Max. Being honest with herself, she was furious with Dillon as well. The battle of wills between her ex and current boyfriend seemed close to critical mass. She wondered how in the world she could keep going on, stuck in the middle, even though there wasn't anything to truly be stuck in. She was with Max.

Only Max, she reassured herself.

Layna thought back to the day he had first noticed her or, truth be told, how she got him to notice her. She'd later find out she didn't have much work to do, as he had already checked her out. Layna and Nancy knew of him from around campus, but mostly from his technical work on the productions the school put on. They never said anything to him, but the two girls were more than aware of how good looking he was.

It was a sunny afternoon on the quad, Layna remembered. It was a Tuesday, she had drama twice that day, instead of only once, when gym replaced the other major slot. She and Nancy ran lines, laughed, and gossiped, when suddenly Max and Crosby stepped into view. The two threw a football back and forth on the grassy quad. Layna found it hard to keep her eyes off Max, whose tanned, muscled body was evident in a blue tank top.

Layna played with her hair a bit more than usual, laughed a little more gregariously, and generally made herself a girl to watch. Nancy was much more obvious in her taste for Crosby. In fact, Layna had to tell her to stop when Nancy stretched one of her long legs over her head while staring directly at her would-be suitor. It worked. He didn't even watch the ball fly toward and right past his face, drooling mouth agape.

The ball landed near the girls, and Layna slapped Nancy on the thigh when her friend said her work was done. Layna knew what she meant. Both boys sauntered over, Crosby to say hello to Nancy, and Max to retrieve the football. When he told Layna he was sorry it had gotten so close, Layna responded that she wasn't, immediately feeling it was too strong a come-on. But, hey, why not, she thought. She certainly didn't flip her hair so he'd ignore her.

After she and Max had a brief conversation about the school having no sports teams, and what they both wanted to do and be, a relationship seemed destined. Lunches together as a foursome, some weekend double dates on the mainland, and then single dates for each couple sealed the deal.

Layna couldn't believe that was only less than a year ago. It had taken her a while to let Max know she had dated Dillon. It wasn't very serious, and Max had nothing to worry about in terms of her remaining friends with her ex. It seemed just fine at first. But maybe Dillon did hang around a little too much, or seem to find her, or bump into her, on more occasions than what might seem coincidental.

She wasn't sure.

She wasn't sure of a lot these last few days.

A bright flash of lightning and a slap of thunder brought her back to the task at hand, which was getting inside the dance studio and, hopefully, finding Nancy. If anyone knew what to say to get her out of what she silently thought of as World War DilMax, Nancy would.

Layna finally reached the building, pulled on the glass doors, and stepped inside. She grabbed her hair to squeeze out the dampness, which didn't do much. She wished she had her umbrella. But who in Seattle really has an umbrella, she thought, which forced her to flash to the images she saw on the dean's desk. Of an umbrella. Of Sydney.

Of death.

Thumping bass music filled Layna's chest and she followed that feeling to the room where Nancy was dancing. Even with such loud music, Layna walked lightly so she would not disturb her friend, not scare her, or distract her in the middle of a routine. Like everyone else, Layna loved to watch Nancy dance. She thought with certainty that her friend would get accepted into a prominent dance company upon graduation. Something in New York. Or maybe even London or Moscow. And Layna knew Nancy deserved it.

Layna made her way to the closed door and watched from behind its slim, vertical pane of glass. On the other side, feeling the heavy beat of the music, she watched Nancy glide effortlessly across the floor. Her kicks were eye level, and the point of her toes and the arch in her feet was perfect. In her pale blue, skintight outfit, her taut, strong body seemed to float and hover for a magical moment. Split-leaps, grand jetés, and fouetté turns took flight. And when it came to turns, there was nothing like watching the girl spin, her head whipping to keep her spot, showcasing a hidden power within her. She finished her multiple rotations as if she were an ice skater at the end of a routine, moving so fast they became a blue blur.

Layna let her mouth hang open in awe. Being an actress was one thing, but watching Nancy dance made Layna understand what hard work really accomplished. The sweat dripping from Nancy was proof that all things were possible when you practiced what you loved.

As Nancy came to a stop, her arms stretched out in a pose Layna read as both, *Thank you, I'm done,* and, *Beat that, bitches.*

"Brava!" Layna said, her hands red from clapping.

Nancy fell out of her pose and screamed at the sight and sound of Layna. The suddenness of the reaction made Layna scream back. The two girls looked at each other, and their screams dulled, turned into smiles, and then broke into laughter.

"Jesus, you scared me!" Nancy said, fanning her face with both hands.

"I scared you? I come in with congratulations and you scream like Freddy Krueger's behind me." Layna grabbed a towel from a nearby rack and threw it to Nancy. "I just wanted to say you look amazing."

Nancy sopped up the moisture on her face and arms. "And you look conflicted. What's up, dare I ask?"

Layna grimaced and tilted her head down, but kept her eyes up. It was her sweet puppy-dog face. "Promise you won't tell me you told me so?"

"As your friend tried and true, I will not promise that," Nancy said, throwing the wet towel in a bin. She sat down on the floor and started to stretch.

Layna sat in front of her and put her feet against her friend's so they could pull one another down, back and forth, stretching together. "It's Max. And Dillon."

"Surprise, surprise," Nancy said, the words coated with sarcasm.

Layna glared.

"What? I didn't say I told you so," Nancy said. "I just thought it. I thought it really, really hard."

Layna yanked her friend forward so her face almost met the floor. Nancy laughed as Layna crossed her legs and arms.

"It's just, Max is acting all alpha male, and Dillon is, well—" Layna searched for the right word.

Nancy finished the thought. "Dillon?"

"Right, whatever that means," Layna agreed. "So I left them to duke it out and came here. Ooh, gossip girl! Max got hauled in by McKenna, which serves him right. And then Dillon went, well, I don't know. Wherever Dillon goes, I guess. It's just too much drama right now."

Nancy smiled as she stood. "Coming from you that means it's a lot of drama." She grabbed her bag and a bottle of water as she and Layna walked out.

Layna wondered if Nancy ever had any real pressures, real difficulties. Other than not wanting to go to the country club with her parents, or staying out past her curfew, her life had been smooth sailing. Nancy came from money, a lot of money. A family in local politics, a brother on the board of a Washington, D.C. charity. It was a nice life if you could get it.

Because, Layna thought, she did not get it. Few people knew she lived with her grandparents after the death of her parents. Layna was not like the other girls at Trask, but she was pretty, and smart, and talented. And that's what mattered. She also didn't know, or care, how much privilege friends like Nancy had come from. But she did know that Nancy felt it made Layna a true friend.

They reached the front door. Nancy turned back to Layna and spoke. "And don't bother asking me to detective out Crosby right now. That's the difficult part of being the magician's assistant," Nancy admitted. "I can't make him appear if I don't know where he is."

Layna was about to laugh, but she screamed and grabbed Nancy, who also screamed. They saw a shadowy figure in the doorway, a frightening silhouette in a flash of lightning. The two girls backed away when the doors opened.

It was Crosby. "Jesus, it's freaking pouring!"

He rushed in, letting a blast of cold, moist air in before the door finally shut itself. He was out of breath. He looked at Nancy, then to Layna. "Wait a minute, aren't you supposed to be at the library?"

Layna shifted her eyes from Crosby to Nancy and back to Crosby. The comment took her by surprise. "Who said I was *supposed* to be anywhere? And how did you know I was at the library?"

Crosby had a lump in his throat instead of an answer. Before he could utter anything, both doors flung open again. Wind and rain skittered in behind Max. He didn't bother to shut the door. He was soaking wet.

Layna stared at him. He looked haggard, frantic. And it seemed to Layna that he had been crying.

"She's dead," he blurted out. "Alice is dead!"

"Dammit, she was right here!" Max yelled.

Water droplets hit the floor as Max, Layna, Crosby, and Nancy stood at the bottom of the main staircase in the library. There was nothing else to see but the rain they brought in with them. The group stared at Max, who ran a hand through his slick hair.

Layna noticed how dark his hair looked when wet, almost like it wasn't a part of the Max she knew. But it was him, and she was worried. She reached her arm out to his, but he pulled away. It was so fast she hoped it was instinct. Hoped his anger was not because of her, but because they weren't seeing what he saw. Or worse, because he thought they didn't believe he'd seen anything at all.

"Are you sure she wasn't playing some sort of joke?" Crosby asked.

Max eyed him with a look of contempt.

"Payback *can* be a bitch," said Nancy, shrugging. "You did get her with that whole ghost story thing. I think it freaked her—"

"Jesus Christ for the tenth time, no!" Max said. "She was lying. Right. Here. There was blood."

His voice trailed off. This time Layna did not allow Max to pull away when she tried to hold him. It was important to her that he know she believed him.

But for a split second she wondered if she did. *Alice? Dead?*

"Somebody moved her after I saw her. That has to be it," Max thought aloud.

Layna stepped away from Max and the group to search for something, anything.

Nancy snickered. "Oh God, I just hate it when someone touches my corpses without asking."

Layna turned when she heard Nancy yelp. Max had grabbed her by both shoulders. This wasn't like Max. At all.

Nancy immediately stopped being silly. Crosby jumped in, Max let Nancy go, and she backed away.

"Hey! Chillax, bro!" Crosby yelled. "Seriously, what's wrong with you?"

Layna stared at Max and felt like he was coming unglued, but then something caught her attention.

Crosby took a breath. "Look, just start from the beginning. Tell us where you were, what you saw, and how—"

Layna rushed back to the group. She was holding something dark in her hand. "Guys, look."

She held it out for all of them to see. And while even she had to admit it might not make any of them believe Max, it should certainly give them pause.

The thing in Layna's hand was hard to recognize. It was matted, tangled, and wet. It had been dunked in something black, thick, and sticky.

"What is that?" Nancy said, almost disgusted.

Layna turned her hand and the thing flopped to one side, where the tiny, glass eyes became visible and stared up at them.

"Oh, my God." Layna felt as if the air had been sucked from her body. She dropped the black blob to the floor where there was no mistaking it.

"It's the head of Alice's keychain."

Inside Daniel's small security office, Max tried to keep his cool as he spoke to Detective Parker. The young man looked through the window to the waiting room. He saw Layna, Crosby, and Nancy as they waited. Though Nancy and Crosby seemed to occupy themselves with idle chatter, Layna was clearly nervous.

Max was nervous, too, and crossed his arms. He hated being in the room with Parker. He hated having to keep Layna and his friends wondering. And he hated having to repeat *Alice is dead* over and over and over.

As Parker spoke, Max glanced at Layna. He could see in her eyes she was desperate to hear every word being said. And though she could not, he knew that, somehow, she knew exactly what was going on.

Max turned his attention back to the detective. He sucked in a deep breath and clenched his fists.

"Listen, again, to what I am telling you. McKenna took me to see you, and when we were done, I went back to my dorm. I remembered Alice still had my bag at the library. I went to get it, and then I found her." Max let his hands relax.

"Dead," Parker said.

"Yes, I told you!" Max yelled.

The detective got up from the chair behind the desk, stood in front of it, and leaned back. Max didn't like him being close, so he took a step back.

"So," Parker said, "what happened to her? Dead girls don't get up and walk away."

Max, tired of going in circles, turned away from Parker, but he felt the detective's eyes boring a hole in his back.

The expression on Max's face, the one he tried to hide from Parker, from Layna, from everyone, was somber and sullen. These feelings rarely touched him, but now they closed in and clenched at his throat. He pushed them aside, perked up, and turned to Parker.

"The keychain. Her stupid keychain," Max said in a revelatory manner.

"The black cat?" Parker asked.

Max shook his head. "She loved that stupid thing and wouldn't go anywhere without it. And it's white, not black. Or it was white. Somebody put ink all over it." Max had figured it out. "Oh my God. Ink! Don't you get it? It's the stuff that numptie Dillon uses to write his sheet music."

Parker squinted. "Stay here," he said as he left.

Max listened through the slightly open door. He watched as Parker was descended upon by Layna and the others.

"Detective, how's Max?" Layna asked.

"And where's Alice," Nancy wondered. She stood, and Crosby did as well.

Daniel had come in from the storm just as Parker rapped on

the office window. Max looked at him and saw the detective motion for him to come out. He did, and welcomed Layna's hug. It cleansed the feeling of being interrogated.

"Alice? Hello? Someone, anyone?" Nancy asked.

"I wasn't able to locate her. Yet," Daniel emphasized.

"There's only so many places she could have gone," Parker offered. "And she could have left the library for any reason. As for you, Max, we're through here. You can go."

Max was relieved and pulled Layna in tighter.

"Pull the file on the Reeves kid," Parker said.

Layna pushed away from Max, hard enough for him to know something was wrong. Nancy and Crosby noticed it, too.

"What?" Max asked loudly.

Layna glared at him, and he knew he was in trouble.

Layna shoved open the exterior doors to the building with both arms. She walked out fast and ran down the stairs. Max tried to catch up.

"Jesus, I cannot believe you!" Layna said, spinning on her heels to face him. The sudden about-face stopped him in his tracks. "Or, you know what? Maybe I can," she added. "I get that you hate him, but for you to open your mouth and literally barf out lies about him?"

Max tried to gently grab her shoulders, but she pulled away. "I wasn't lying," he said.

Layna jostled back and forth, agitated. "It wasn't the truth! We don't know what's going on. But you took the first opportunity to set Dillon up. Why would you do that?"

"Because I know exactly what's going on. Alice is dead," Max said.

Layna saw that he was on the verge of breaking. Her expression softened, but she was still angry. Still confused.

"Technically, she's just missing," Nancy said coming down the steps. Crosby was beside her.

Layna pulled her head back at the cavalier statement. She thought everyone was acting crazy, but this didn't sound like Nancy. And Crosby, she noticed, seemed oddly calm.

"Shut up, Nancy. She's dead," Max said with concrete certainty. "I. Saw. Her."

"And, what, you saw Dillon *kill* her?" Layna asked. "Max, you sound insane! Dillon would never do that. And Alice, dammit, I don't know."

Crosby broke in. "This is going nowhere. Can we just calm down?"

Layna stumbled back as she watched Max explode in a fury. Spittle came from his lips as he yelled, his face and ears turning red. She had never seen him like this before.

"She's dead! Some bastard murdered her!" Max wiped his mouth with his sleeve. Layna didn't know what to do for him as he backed away. She felt torn, and when his eyes welled up with tears, she was sure they would break if he blinked.

"I'm sorry. I'm sorry. I just—don't know," Max said. Then he turned and ran into the night. A wisp of cool, moist air swirled behind him.

Layna put her hands to her face as Nancy stepped up beside her.

Crosby pursed his lips and kept looking in the direction Max had disappeared. "I'm seriously worried about him. I think he needs a checkup from the neck up."

Layna pulled away from Nancy. "Come on."

Nancy didn't hide her quizzical, sarcastic tone. "Um, to

where? More crazy?"

Layna stepped ahead of them down the wet pavement. Nancy grabbed Crosby's hand and dragged him behind.

"Alice didn't just disappear," Layna called back to them.

Nancy skipped a few beats ahead of Crosby and turned around to him, walking backward near Layna as she spoke. "If she did, maybe she can help you learn how to do it?"

Layna didn't care to look at Nancy or Crosby. She didn't care what they said or did and certainly had no time to mention their casual attitude, or what she perceived as callousness. Layna decided right then she was going to do three things.

She was going to find Alice.

She was going to find Dillon.

And she was going to find out what really happened.

CHAPTER VIII

Layna led her friends to the library once again, though there was no need to huddle around the still empty foyer. Alice was not there.

Layna avoided the subject so as to not begin another round of verbal blows with Max. The ice they were on was already thin enough because of Sydney's dreadful act, the tension between Dillon and Max, and now Alice.

"*The Disappearance of Alice.* It sounds like the title of an awesome YA novel," Crosby said, as they made their way to the building's research room.

Nancy walked beside him. "If there's a Lifetime movie based on her, I hope they make her a dancer so I can call dibs on playing her."

Layna shook her head. She didn't understand their playful attitudes, and she didn't want to hear them. She looked around, but everything seemed to be in its place. Everything seemed to be just fine. *Except Alice isn't here*, she thought. *Everything is not fine.*

"Guys, wait a sec," Nancy said. "Come over here." She stood in front of a stack, her face inches from the books.

Layna rushed to her and realized there were small gashes in the spines of the books, probably not noticeable unless you were looking for something out of the ordinary. If even one of the books had been missing, or placed upside down, the thin line of jagged tearing might have gone unseen, or dismissed as kids being careless with the library's property.

But this was nothing like that. Not at all.

"A knife did that," Layna said. She frowned and looked at Max, then reached for his hand and was glad when he took it.

Nancy ran her fingers over the scratches, then pulled them back and rubbed them together to get rid of any lingering dust. She stepped back from the stacks and looked at the others. "Deputy Danny either didn't see this—"

"Or he's lying," Layna offered. She looked to Max. She now knew his story made sense, at least some of it.

"I'll tell you, I'm on board the *I officially do not like this* train," Crosby muttered. "Something's wrong."

He took the silver coin out of his pocket and ran it around his fingers. Layna knew it would keep his mind from wandering to the terrible things that she also hoped not to think about.

Blood.

Alice.

Death.

"I told you!" Max startled everyone, especially Layna. She and the others ran over to him. He knelt next to the computer desk where Alice had worked. He held something in his hand.

"What's that?" Nancy asked, beating Layna to it.

Max swallowed hard and took a breath. He pointed to the outlet. It was a wreck. Small black marks trailed off the white plug cover where electricity had arced from the force of the cord being torn out. He held up the plug. It was intact, but its prongs were twisted oddly.

Layna knelt next to Max and placed a hand on his knee for support. Max's free hand went to hers, and Layna felt lighter when the weight of worry about the things unsaid between her and her boyfriend lifted, at least temporarily.

Nancy and Crosby stayed back. They were done being cavalier, but Layna could see they had questions.

Nancy spoke first. "Listen, I see it. I get it. Weird? Check. But we're not any closer to finding out what actually happened to Alice."

Max stood up. "At least you now know something happened."

Layna was worried that there might be another argument when Nancy retorted, "Yeah, something happened. Or she went somewhere in a hurry. Look, I don't know."

"You do know," Max said, defiant. "You just can't deal."

"I didn't see what you said you saw," Nancy spat back. "There, I said it."

Layna stared at the printer. She looked on top of it, and around it. She crouched down and wriggled her arm behind the heavy desk as best she could. Her face scrunched up as she strained. Something was back there. Her eyes squinted as she pushed her arm as far as it would go, which was not much more than below her elbow. But then her eyes widened. She got it.

"Don't act like I don't care about her, because I do," Nancy said.

"When you stop acting like you don't, I'll be good," Max snapped back.

"Guys," Crosby pleaded. "Please."

"Oh my God," Layna said, reading the piece of paper she had found, her head shaking.

"Well?" Crosby demanded.

Layna's arm dropped to her side. She said nothing. She could say nothing. The words wouldn't come.

Max grabbed the paper from Layna's hand and scanned it. She watched as his eyes darted back and forth.

"Jesus, tell us!" Nancy said.

Layna didn't expect Max's response.

"Who are you?" he asked, looking right into Layna's eyes.

She looked back at him, empty inside. The words stuck in the back of her throat, thick as mucus. She went numb, the tingling starting at the bottom of her feet and traveling up the length of her body. She had to shake her head to keep from succumbing to the black and white dots sizzling in her vision.

"My mother—" Layna uttered, the rest of the sentence clinging to the inside of her mouth, as if not saying it would keep it untrue. "My mother went to school here."

Max stared at her, looking confused.

Nancy's mouth hung open.

The coin in Crosby's hand stopped moving and dropped to the floor with a soft thunk.

"You told us you didn't know your mother," Crosby said, with more than a tinge of accusation.

Layna was stung as she looked at them. She could feel them wondering what other secrets she was hiding, though she wasn't hiding anything at all. She wanted to say something, anything, to defend herself. But the words did not come.

Instead, Nancy spoke. "Try working on your whole inside voice staying inside thing, Cros."

Crosby ignored her and picked up his coin. He shoved it in his pocket.

Layna regained composure. "I didn't know her." She looked right at Max. "I don't. But this reference sheet says she went here. And she wrote a play." Layna thought silently for a moment, then walked away.

As she made her way outside the library, she dashed through the falling rain with purpose. Her face glistened every time she passed a lamppost.

Max and the others kept up with her quick pace.

Layna kept her eyes forward as she spoke to them, answering the unasked questions she knew must have swirled in their minds. "You're not getting it."

"Evidently not," Nancy said.

Layna stopped. She took a deep breath. She saw in the distance the old, burned theater, its construction material covered in tarps that flapped in the wind. She centered herself and looked each of her companions in the eye. She had to make them see why this was a big deal.

"My grandparents told me my mother died in a car accident when I was a baby," Layna said. "Why would they say that?"

"Maybe they didn't know?" Crosby offered, half-hearted.

Nancy practically snorted. "Idiot, they'd know. They were *lying*. Besides, parents don't forget writing checks to this place. I know. I never hear the end of it."

"Yeah, but no one is writing checks for the scholarship girl. Maybe there's a reason why?" Crosby said.

That hurt Layna.

Max took a step toward her, but she wriggled away from him.

"I need to find a phone," she said. "Or Mrs. D. I want some damn answers."

"I know you're upset," Max said, "but we should stick together, especially after—"

Nancy jumped in. "He's right. Until we find Alice."

Max clenched his jaw. "I *saw* her."

"Max, please stop it," Crosby said. "We've had enough stories about dead people."

Max paid no mind. "I tried to help her," he said. "I thought she might have even been breathing. She was killed."

"Stop it," Crosby said forcefully.

Nancy looked physically uncomfortable. But Max did not stop. Layna watched him with a look of pity.

"All the blood," Max said. "They left her there and came back to get her."

"I said shut up! Shut up! Shut up!" Crosby exploded.

Layna felt the tension as a tangible thing, like sheets of mist that hung in the air after a rain. If it were colder, they would freeze, drop to the ground, and shatter.

"Okay, Max, we're listening," Nancy said calmly. "But it's hard to picture. It must have been a joke. I mean, why in the world would anyone kill anyone here? And Alice? I mean, for God's sake, it's Alice!"

There was no easy answer for that. And Layna knew it. As she sucked in a breath to form the words in her mind, Crosby was already talking, the obviousness of a theory dawning on his face.

"She was helping you," he said.

The statement did not shock Layna, nor did it offend. It was what she had been thinking but was afraid to say.

Crosby went on. "What Alice found, maybe nobody knew. I mean somebody knew, but I don't think anybody was ever really supposed to know."

"But if she found this, then she knew," Max added. "And now she's, well, she's gone."

Nancy shivered. "Creepy."

Layna wasted no time in heading off a theory which had not occurred to her until her friends weaved bits and pieces of information into a cloth of which she wanted no part. "Wait. This is not my fault," she said.

"Nobody said that," Max offered, but the look on his face suggested that he might have thought otherwise. And in that instant, Layna hated him for it.

"Forget that," Crosby stated. "We have to figure out what to do next."

Layna had the answer. She looked at Nancy. "You look for Alice. She has to be here, somewhere. And Max, fine, go watch Dillon if you can."

Crosby's eyes were wide open. "What about me?"

Layna continued, grabbing his arm. "We're going to the archives."

"Wait, why?" Crosby asked.

"You're the writer. You have keys to the building."

"So," Crosby countered.

Layna examined the faces of her friends as they stared at her. She wondered whether everything in life would come to arguments. To secrets and lies.

Death.

"So," she said with certainty, "there's a play I'm dying to read."

CHAPTER IX

Nancy led Max as they snuck around the campus security office. The lights were on, but Daniel was not inside. She let out a breath. "All clear."

"Okay, Nancy Drew," Max said.

Nancy peeked behind the desk. The computer's screensaver was on, so she knew Daniel had recently been there. "Deputy Danny is on the prowl."

"I feel safer already," Max added.

Nancy liked Daniel. All the kids on campus did. He was nice and sweet and never went too far with punishment. At least in students' minds, he was the opposite of McKenna. Daniel was also cute. Nancy threw the thought off and went back to focusing on their task. "What I wanna know is, where is Detective Parker?"

Max shrugged as he picked up the desk telephone. "What I do know is we don't wanna wait until Monday for the next ferry ..." His voice trailed off. "What? No way."

Nancy watched as he clicked the receiver.

"The phone's dead," he said.

Nancy grabbed the phone. "That's ridiculous—"

She heard nothing. No dial tone. No static. She clicked the receiver, and with every click, she felt her heart beat faster.

Nancy pulled the phone away from her ear, staring at Max, hoping he'd have an answer. Hoping that whatever he was going to say next would calm her heart and force the hairs on the back of her neck and arms to stand down.

But Max stood silent.

Nancy shifted her weight from foot to foot. "What does that mean?"

"It means we're stuck on this island."

The archives, Crosby thought, had started to feel more and more like the school itself: shockingly beautiful and near-perfect on the outside, but severe, cold, and hollow inside.

The exterior was made of well-laid brick and stone, and a carved staircase led up to heavy wooden doors with leaded glass. The small windows did not allow anyone to peer in. Crosby surmised that the archives were another monument to the formality and power the school exuded almost sickeningly.

Crosby walked in front of Layna and put his access key in the lock. The door opened. He looked at Layna as if to ask whether or not this was really what she wanted to do. When she nodded, he led her inside.

"This looks like an old warehouse," Layna said.

"What did you expect, the Ritz?" Crosby asked.

"Um kinda, I guess."

"Have you never been in here before?"

"I'm an actor. My research is on the streets, not on shelves."

Crosby stopped. "Oh my god, please do not make me barf."

Layna laughed. "I'm totally kidding. But, no, I've never been in here. It's certainly chock full of whatever it's chock full of."

Crosby started moving again, and Layna followed. He never thought about how packed the place was or, frankly, of what it was mostly packed. He always went for old papers and stories and general research. As a writer, that's what he did, or at least what he thought he was supposed to do. But, he silently agreed, the place was kind of a mess.

He and Layna continued past layers of shelving, rows of file cabinets, and dust. It was no secret that the building's innards looked less than perfect. Far from it. Everyone on campus whose work included in-depth research was aware. However, the contents of the archived memos, files, papers, scripts, and whatever else Trask Academy of Performing Arts kept lying around, were mostly a secret. One did not get entrance keys lightly, but studious and trusted students could.

Students like me, Crosby thought.

Now he wondered if those keys would be taken away. He wondered what they were looking for as he stared at the printout in Layna's hand. He wondered. And he worried. About what they might find. Or what might find them.

"Here," Layna said, turning down a long stretch of filing cabinets. More than a few had boxes stacked on top of them, filing for student workers to handle that was clearly not being handled.

Layna ran a finger against the cool metal of the cabinets, one by one. She slowed her pace and then stopped in front of one, staring at it as if she were waiting for it to greet her.

Crosby waited, then grimaced. "Earth to Layna, what's the sitch?"

But Layna remained focused straight ahead. She spoke in a hushed tone. "This is it," she said. "It's in here."

The look on her face seemed to ask for permission, guidance, something. Crosby decided to give it to her. He stepped between her and the cabinet and opened the drawer. Dust swirled in small vortices, and they both coughed and waved it away.

"I've never been this deep," Crosby admitted. "What are they hiding here? Death?" He immediately regretted the words. "Sorry."

Layna shook it off and began flipping through files. "It's

okay."

As she worked her fingers through faded manila envelopes, yellowing paper, and tattered hanging green folders, Crosby kept an eye out. He fidgeted and strolled in small circles. He grabbed his coin and guided it through his fingers. The large fluorescent lights above reminded him of the lights from the gymnasium in his public middle school. He hated them then, and he hated them now, especially their incessant buzzing. He wanted to get out of there. "It doesn't make any sense. Why hide that your mom was a student here? Who would care? And who knew about—"

"Found it!" Layna yelled. Her voice reverberated slightly through the building's expanse and made Crosby jump.

"Jesus Christ, don't do that!" he said to her.

"This," Layna said, clutching something to her chest. "This is it."

Layna put the material on top of the files in the open cabinet so Crosby could get a good look.

He wasn't sure what to expect, but the stained, shabby manuscript, with its three-holed paper bound with just one tarnished brass brad in the upper-left corner, seemed something of a letdown.

Until he saw the words on the cover. Words created with old school typewriter ink:

JINXED

a play in three acts by Amanda Kincaid

"No way," he said. There it was, written by the woman Layna never knew, the woman no one knew, the woman who never went to school at Trask. Layna flipped through it voraciously, but Crosby felt compelled to leave. "Great, you've got it. Can we look at it somewhere else? Like, anywhere that's not here?" There was an urgency in his tone.

Layna remained engrossed in the words, her fingers moving from page to page, her eyes from phrase to phrase.

"Hello," Crosby said. "I've decided creepy is not in season, but somehow we're standing in the middle of it. Let's. Go." He reached for Layna's arm.

She pulled away, her eyes not veering from their down position. "Just gimme a second!"

Crosby huffed. He kept quiet, looked around, and then pointed at his wrist as if he wore a watch. He cleared his throat once, but Layna did nothing. He cleared it again, louder, and she looked up at him quizzically. "My pretend watch is telling me it's time to get out of here for real," he said.

Layna shook her head. "Fine, I get it." She grabbed the manuscript. "Is there anything else in the file?"

Crosby looked into the drawer as fast as humanly possible. "Nope! Time to go." He readied to leave, but Layna didn't budge. He saw she was confused. Hurt. "What's wrong?" he asked.

"The last act of the play. It's missing."

Crosby marched back and slammed shut the file cabinet drawer with a loud clang. "And, we're done," he said. "Let's go."

They did just that. Layna led the way, and Crosby watched as she clung to the manuscript with her small hands. "We need to find the others, and fast," he said. The tone of his voice was full of worry, though he tried to mask it.

Layna slowed and turned toward him. She stayed silent, but the look on her face let Crosby know that she was worried, too.

He nodded, and just wanted them to get out of there.

Then, he stopped. He held his arm out to stop Layna and put a finger to his lips. His eyes went wide, then the same finger went to his ear.

They were not alone.

Crosby craned his neck to listen to the voices. There were two people, whispering. He pulled Layna back from the main walkway. The two of them stood tall and straight against the shelves behind them as the hushed voices carried through the great building, getting closer.

And closer.

The tall shadows of two people stretched across the ground, nearing where Crosby and Layna stood. Crosby could not yet make out the voices, nor could he decipher what they said. But the secrecy with which they spoke worried him.

He turned his head back the way they had come and squinted. He kept his voice as quiet as possible. "We're stuck. Even if we ran, they'd see us before we turned a corner."

The shadows of the interlopers were close enough to touch. Worry forced blood into Crosby's head. His cheeks and ears turned red and hot. But then he listened more carefully to the voices. Not to the words, but the cadence, the pitch, the sound.

And he knew. He looked at Layna and saw it did not escape her, either. Her expression crinkled. His became tighter. Layna pulled away from him.

"No," Crosby whispered to her, but Layna did not listen. She tiptoed out from hiding and came face to face with—

"Mrs. D.?" Layna asked, surprised.

"And Dillon," Crosby added. He should have recognized the deeper, huskier voice of Layna's ex.

The teacher stepped back, startled. Dillon stood as if nothing out of the ordinary were going on. His eyes locked on Layna.

Mrs. D. dropped her arm. "Layna, Crosby, what—"

"Are we doing here?" Crosby finished for her. "It's so funny you'd ask that."

"Yeah, because we have the same exact question for you two," Layna added.

"There are a few things Dillon and I need," D'Arcangelo said.

Crosby stepped forward and trained his gaze on her. He wasn't the least bit interested in whether the elder woman liked him. Frankly, he wondered if she even really knew him. He wasn't one of her students and wasn't even in her department.

"From the writer's archives?" Crosby snickered. "What are you doing? Putting together your less-than-anticipated autobiography?" It struck him immediately that the comment may have been too much, too nasty, when he saw D'Arcangelo was flustered, perhaps embarrassed.

"Crosby, stop," Layna chided.

Crosby offered no apology. "You know," he said, stepping toward Dillon, "I'd love to hear where you were earlier tonight? Hmm? I don't know, let me guess? Maybe the library? Have you seen Alice, by chance?"

Crosby knew he couldn't take Dillon in a fight, but he saw Dillon flinch.

"That's enough," D'Arcangelo said. "Our being here doesn't concern you, Crosby."

Dammit. She knows me.

"Calm yourself down, and leave Mr. Reeves alone," D'Arcangelo went on. "As for you, Layna, you don't look well. I'm sorry we startled you, but we were, as you plainly heard, not necessarily working hard to keep our presence in this building a secret. From you, or anybody else. Now tell me what's going on. What's all this about? Are you all right?"

"No, I'm not," Layna said. "Alice is missing."

Crosby studied Dillon, who looked like a stone effigy. Cold and unfeeling.

"What do you mean, missing?" D'Arcangelo asked.

"We mean totally gone," Crosby jumped in. "Layna and Max were with Alice at the library. They left her to get some food and no one has seen Alice since."

"She was helping me look for a piece for the showcase," Layna said. "Apparently she found something and disappeared. The next person who saw her was Max. But he said—"

Crosby hoped Layna wouldn't say it. The unspoken words hung heavy.

"What? What did your ever-loving, all-knowing boyfriend say?" Dillon wondered aloud, no longer hiding his disdain.

Crosby stepped forward, practically spitting the words. "He said Alice was dead. Murdered. Covered in blood."

The words shut Dillon up as Crosby knew they would.

D'Arcangelo's face turned ashen. "Dear God, what are you saying?"

"We don't know for sure. No one else saw her but Max," Layna said. "But what she found, we found. A play, Mrs. D."

"Written by someone very special. Someone very unexpected," Crosby added.

D'Arcangelo shook her head, and Crosby realized she wasn't following.

"Written by my *mother*," revealed Layna.

If there were color left in the older woman's face, it would have drained, Crosby thought. He watched as Layna kept her head down as she spoke.

"I know, not possible, right? I mean, how could I have found a play at this school when my mother never went here?"

The last words were thrown in D'Arcangelo's direction, along with a look that seemed to tell the woman that Layna may never listen to her again. Crosby knew that would be tough for the teacher to bear.

Crosby looked at Dillon, who seemed to be filled with something he had never seen in him before. Was it pity? Sorrow? Or maybe he was reflecting some of the sad and worried feelings

Layna had given off.

Ultimately, Crosby didn't know, and didn't care.

Layna went on, her voice rising. "That would make my mother's dying just after I was born either pretty impossible or the best magic trick this side of Penn and freaking Teller, wouldn't you say, Cros?"

Crosby grabbed Layna's arm for support and was surprised when she pulled away.

"Did you know?" she asked, moving closer to D'Arcangelo.

The teacher didn't answer right away, so Layna stepped forward.

"Layn, hey," Crosby said, ready to step in.

"I'm going to ask one more time," Layna uttered coldly, looking directly at D'Arcangelo. "Did. You. Know?"

The color returned to D'Arcangelo's face. "Of course not," she said. "But I think we need to sit down and talk about this in private."

Layna's tongue clicked against the roof of her mouth, and she swung her head from side to side. "Uh-uh. No more private. No more secrets. You wanna know why? Because I finally found a piece of material, a play, that means something to me. And I'm not going to stop until I get to the bottom of it."

Grabbing Crosby's hand, Layna pulled him to leave. As the two walked away, Crosby did not look back, and he knew Layna would not, either.

"I really hope this school is ready!" Layna called out.

CHAPTER X

Max and Nancy ran through the empty paths of the campus and wiped rain from their faces as they dodged puddles and thick, sticky mud. The two of them rushed to McKenna's residence. It was inside the confines of the campus gates, but far enough away that it felt as if it were outside the school's reach.

Nancy panted and huffed as she watched Max overtake her lead. She had stamina, but Max was bigger, stronger, faster, and the rain wasn't helping her. In fact, neither were the wind and the chill it was bringing. Each time a burst of lightning flashed, or thunder boomed, she flinched. She certainly wasn't afraid of a storm, but now of all times, it did not ease her nerves. Not after Alice went missing. Not after the phones went out.

Max suddenly stopped. Nancy tried to as well but slid on wet grass, stopping only when she grabbed on to Max. Even then he did not turn to her. Did not flinch. She let go and stood next to him as he looked around.

"Dammit, where is it?" Max asked.

"It's around here, I know it." Nancy sounded more confident than she really should have. She tried to gauge their location in the darkness. "We passed the commissary and the transpo building. There isn't much left but trees and his house."

Another arc of lightning struck the island, illuminating the outline of a cottage through the rain and trees in the distance.

"There," she said, pointing.

Max wiped moisture off his face, but it was immediately replenished with fresh drops of rain. He squinted, but Nancy knew he wasn't seeing it. She used her hands to guide his face.

"Straight ahead," she muttered. "There's a light on. Or something."

Max nodded. "Yeah, or something," he repeated. "Let's go."

This time Max moved slower, and Nancy was glad to be able to walk at his side. They reached the cottage in under a minute. A light was on, but the curtains were drawn so they couldn't see inside.

The two made their way onto the wraparound porch that offered a respite from the storm. Nancy appreciated that the building did not have the outward grandeur of the rest of the campus, but she could tell it was not ill-appointed, either. It was a cabin made of thick, dark logs. The windows were large and trimmed with a rustic bark treated with a dark green wash.

They arrived at the front door where their feet skimmed a burlap welcome mat.

"Do we knock?" Nancy asked.

"Do we care?" Max put his hand on the brushed metal door handle.

Nancy wasn't surprised at his forwardness, not after what he said he'd been through. Still, she would have knocked.

It didn't matter. The doorknob wouldn't turn. Max tried again, harder, but it barely gave.

"Locked," he said. He slammed his fist into the door, making Nancy twitch.

"Great, the one time we need the dean, he isn't around," Nancy said. "What does it matter? He can barely find his ass from his elbow, so what's he gonna do for us?"

Max jumped down from the porch. "I'm not interested in him."

"Then what're we doing here?" Nancy asked.

Max stepped back. Nancy noticed he had something in his hand. Dark and dripping. A rock, covered in thin trails of mud. "We don't want him. We want what he has," Max said, lobbing the rock from hand to hand.

"Max, don't," Nancy warned.

"Stand back."

Nancy didn't. She glared at him, eyebrows raised, hands in front of her, and shoulders shrugged in a questioning manner.

"Fine," Max said. He reared his hand back and pitched the rock through one of the small plate-glass windows of the door. The impact wasn't a surprise to Nancy, but she squealed nonetheless.

After the rock hit the floor, rolled, and stopped, the two of them stood silent and motionless. They listened. After a few seconds, Max looked at Nancy and then turned to the door. She watched as he reached through the shattered hole, worried he would cut himself on the jagged shards that stuck out. He didn't, and he had his jacket to thank.

With his hand inside, Max fiddled to unlock the door and the deadbolt. The thick steel mechanism gave with a slow, heavy thunk.

When the door opened, the two were greeted with a welcome rush of warm air. They were wet and cold and, if they were being honest with themselves, a little scared.

The cottage was less spectacular than Nancy had expected. In fact, it gave her pause. Did McKenna live so sparsely? Aside from furnishings and lamps, obviously Craftsman inspired and well-maintained, the living space had little to offer. It did not scream money, but it did give off an egomaniacal flare she could feel. There wasn't a lot, but what was there was enough to let people know it was *his*.

Nancy saw a lamp on a nearby desk. Just as she was about to

turn it on, Max grabbed her hand.

"We have bigger problems than another light being on," Nancy said, motioning to the glass on the floor.

"That can't be seen a hundred feet away. Your fear of the dark will," Max pointed out.

"I'm not afraid of the dark," Nancy snorted. She took her finger and ran it along the desk, stopping when it hit the edge of a manila folder hidden under a pile of papers and invoices. It struck her because it was the only manila folder. Without moving it from its place, she delicately lifted the open end to get a glimpse of whatever she could spy. When she saw the name, her eyes bulged and her mouth hung open.

Layna Curtis.

A million different things went through Nancy's mind, not the least of which was that the dean of Trask could have a file on anyone or no one, and it shouldn't seem odd. But the fact he had a file on the one student that was, at the moment, at the center of whatever was going on, didn't seem right. It was too perfect. It screamed that McKenna knew more than he ever told anyone. Certainly more than he ever told Layna. The question was, who else knew whatever he did?

"Dude," Nancy said to Max, keeping her eyes down as she tried to leave the folder looking untouched, "something bad is going on. Like, *Game of Thrones* Cersei-after-being-shamed bad."

"I won't argue with you," Max replied. "Believe me or don't believe me. Alice was murdered. Layna found out her childhood was a lie. Call me Sherlock, but somebody wants to make sure we don't know what we know."

Nancy was finally starting to accept as true what he had said all along. She wished he was wrong. Wished she had more time to feel something other than anger, or fear, at what might be going on. Had the events been a movie, she and the others probably would have loved it. But it wasn't a movie. And it was their lives being thrown into chaos.

It was all too much.

"Without cells, and if the phones don't work, McKenna has to have something here in case of an emergency," Max stated.

As he continued to search, Nancy eyed the thick, curled, black wire of a handset snaking up to a closed credenza. "Like a radio."

Max rushed over as Nancy grabbed the rollaway partition of the desk and lifted. It gave way with little effort.

The relief, they both saw, was short-lived, if it existed at all. There was a CB radio. But it had been broken, smashed to pieces.

"Oh, God," Nancy said.

Max traced the edge of where the desk would normally have locked and saw that it had been pried open, and not neatly. Flecks of colored wire stuck out madly where the cord had been ripped from the docking station. Small pieces of black and gray plastic lay around it. The LED screen had spider web cracks in its slightly green glass.

"Dammit," Max said. He turned to Nancy and locked eyes with her. "Now. Now, will you believe me?"

The worried look on Nancy's face told him she did. What it did not tell him was whether or not he was one of the people she should be worried about.

Layna sat on the bed in her dorm room. It was a pleasant space, certainly more luxe than what most people expected of a student's room at school. The walls above a white chair rail were painted a deep blue. Below it, eggshell white. Her bed had a large, fluffy duvet. It was currently crumpled up around her, making it look as though half her body was lost in a sea of swirling, baby blue fabric.

Crosby sat next to her, watching Layna stare down at the manuscript in her hands. She gripped it tightly, as if it might slip away.

"I have to read this," Layna whispered, bringing her eyes to Crosby's.

"Right now?" Crosby wondered.

Layna shook the manuscript ever so lightly. "This connects me to my mom. It's a tangible thing I not only never knew about, but that I was apparently never supposed to find. Maybe it'll help explain what happened to her and why I never knew her."

Layna saw the look of understanding on Crosby's face fade slightly.

"You're going to use it for the showcase, aren't you?" he asked. "It makes sense, I mean, I get it."

"Oh, Cros, not the point," she said, with a bit too much force. She softened. "I don't even care about the showcase anymore. None of us should. Alice found this, and now she's gone. There's something in this play, and I have to figure it out."

Layna watched him for a response, some spark or indication she was making sense, even if nothing going on around them did.

"I'm sorry. I'm being selfish," Crosby said.

Layna grabbed his hand, but he pulled away and stood up. That was the moment she thought, *he doesn't get it.* He *was* being selfish. It was also the first time she wondered whether or not he could be trusted.

"I think it would be best for you to stay here," Crosby stated. "I'm gonna go find Nancy and Max."

"Are you sure?" Layna asked.

Crosby laughed. "Not really, you know. But I'm also gonna see if there's anything else I can find out about your mom. I mean, now we know her name. And your name, kinda."

He started to smile, but Layna watched it fade as he headed for the door.

"Hey, wait."

Crosby turned, and Layna pushed aside her feelings of worry for the moment and enveloped him in a hug. She was glad he returned the embrace.

"Thank you," she said.

"Whatever happens," stated Crosby, "I don't blame you. None of us do."

Layna had never considered that to be an issue. How could it be? The words and power behind them stung her as she pulled away from him. Briefly, the friend she knew as Crosby was gone. Before she could say anything, he had walked out into the hallway.

Layna was now alone, though in those last few moments, she could have sworn she felt emptier in Crosby's embrace.

She locked the deadbolt on the door then stood with her back against it, thinking, *Am I to blame? Am I?*

She looked around her room at the desk full of papers, the shelf of books, the stuffed animals, and the throw pillows on the floor. Thunder and lightning reared their heads outside as her eyes settled back onto her bed where the manuscript lay.

It waited.

It called to her.

It was desperate to be read.

Layna resisted no longer. She went to it, tearing into its first page with a hunger for, and a fear of, the truths it would reveal.

CHAPTER XI

Lillian D'Arcangelo walked the long hallway of the administration building. Her sensible heels clicked on the glossy marble floor. She slowed as she made her way to a glass case that shielded merits, awards, and accolades Trask wanted to show off. As she sat staring at the papers and plaques that had less to do with the school as an institution of learning than with things that praised the school's founder and honored its current keeper Harlan McKenna, she wondered if all of it wasn't at the expense of students.

As Lillian stared into a space so full but so empty, her eyes refocused to her own reflection. She looked at the dark hair she always kept up and thought how much easier it would be to keep it down at her waist, where she felt it belonged. She saw the lines in her face and remembered when she was a student at Trask, so many years ago. She, too, had the same dreams as so many of the girls she now mentored. But it was her eyes she noticed the most, and that filled her with regret. The sadness she hoped only she could see. The melancholy that she hadn't lived a life, but a lie.

Most of the girls, just like herself, would never make it. Some would, of course. Maybe not big, but they'd find work in commercials, or local theater, maybe bit parts in bad Saturday night sci-fi creature features. They'd find a way to make ends meet, maybe by waiting tables, or whip-creaming lattes, or folding T-shirts at a department store while they danced in a theme park, or sang in a club, or played bad parts in bad student films, or painted portraits. She wondered just how long they would hold on to a dream. How long before they grasped that the real world required real money, and a real job, and real responsibility? Those are the tenets that dashed the hopes of so many.

Like me, she had to admit to herself.

The woman knew her story was not one to be told to build up such hope. She was one who couldn't. And because she couldn't, she taught. She made sure her story was kept not just close to her vest, but tucked away inside a deep pocket. No one wanted to mourn the lost career of a fading wannabe. A has-been. She stopped herself from forming the full thought, *a never-was*. She smirked.

She had not given up.

She had given in.

She knew what they said, everyone who couldn't understand what a creative soul is tortured with. The ones who call out the correct sports play minutes after it happens on the field because they, after all, are safe in their recliners with a beer, chips, and a belly.

No one can understand what it's like to lose the one thing you worked for your whole life.

She thought of Sydney, and how the pressure had overtaken her. And then she saw the hurt in Layna's eyes when she was told she'd been given a wonderful opportunity at the expense of another student. Her friend. But the show must go on. That's what they'd been told all their lives.

Lillian knew the cliché was true. Besides, there was a school to run, and students still there who mattered, and expected things. No matter who got hurt.

It made her wonder. It made her worry.

The click of a closing door stopped her from traveling further into the rabbit hole of regret and fear of the place that might be causing such darkness. Its latch entered the strike plate and echoed.

She thought the sound may have originated in her office, so she walked toward it.

Her usually strong fingers tentatively grabbed the brushed metal handle of her door. She knew two things, the first being that she had locked her door, as she always did. It was the second that bothered her, and that was she expected the door handle to lower with ease instead of stopping after her first gentle push.

Her door was locked.

It was also slightly ajar.

She nudged it open. Normally her hand would reach to the left of the door, slide in between a tall filing cabinet and the wall, and flick on the lights. This time she let the hallway fluorescent flood the room, making her a silhouette to the person seated in her chair, who swiveled around to look up at her.

"What are you doing in my office?" she asked McKenna, with more than a little anger in her voice. She watched as the dean, unfazed, scanned the items on her desk.

"We have some things to talk about, you and I," McKenna answered.

Lillian's heart beat fast, and her hands tingled. Adrenaline pumped through her body. She was angry, but also worried.

"It seems there have been some unexpected developments," McKenna stated.

A profound understatement. "Are you kidding me?" she hissed. "None of this would have been an issue had she just been made aware of her mother."

"Careful, Lillian." The dean stood. "Poor Layna and her mother. A tragedy, really. But what of everything else? Hmm? Just where should we draw the line?"

Lillian slammed the door and rushed closer to him. "Lines have been obliterated! First Sydney, and now Alice. We don't know where that poor girl is or what might have happened to her."

"Tragedies are inevitable," the dean said in his smooth, cold voice.

"Just as inevitable as a young girl finding out that the story of her family, her life, has been a lie? Nothing can go right from here." Lillian leaned in toward McKenna. Facing off. "You've dug yourself a grave with these secrets."

The dean raised his right eyebrow before slowly turning to the frosted windows behind the desk.

Lillian watched him. He was so calculated, so calm.

"Is that so?" McKenna asked.

The rhetorical nature of the question was not lost on Lillian. She'd had enough. She wasn't prepared for his tenor, so deep, so dark, more devoid of feeling than she remembered him being capable of. She didn't like what had happened. What was happening. Didn't like what she had been asked to be a part of all these years.

Most of all, for the first time, Lillian D'Arcangelo did not trust her boss, a man she had thought was a friend.

Layna was enveloped by the blankets on her bed, staring at the manuscript. She read each page, then discerned that she had absorbed none of the words, none of the information, none of its meaning. Like it would so often do when she was reading for school, her mind wandered. Her eyes scanned every syllable, but they ultimately meant nothing, and she would have to re-read them.

Layna was far too young, a baby, to remember her mother, but the two had been together. Or so she was told. Her grandparents, her mother's parents, had mentioned the times Amanda took her for walks in the park when the air was cool and crisp. Or that Layna would be seated in the baby carrier, facing her mother, and that they couldn't stop looking at one another and smiling.

Reading the pages, their difficult words about revenge, prejudice, and tolerance, and yes, murder, was difficult. But more difficult was that everything Layna ever thought she knew may not have been true. The adults entrusted to care for and love and shape her could no longer be trusted. Her grandparents were the chief offenders. Why had they allowed a charade to go on so long? Why—how—could they smile even as they lied to their only grandchild? And Mrs. D'Arcangelo, to whom Layna looked up, was now part of some master plan to sweep secrets not just under a rug, but away forever. What she and Dean McKenna had not counted on was that there was always a time when things must come clean.

Layna stopped in mid-flip of a page when a noise, something she couldn't quite make out, rattled from somewhere in the hallway. She looked up to the left wall of her room, where it seemed to be the loudest.

Definitely in the hallway, she thought. Definitely close.

Her eyes went to the deadbolt on her door, and she let out a small breath when she saw it was locked. She waited silently, her head up, her mouth slightly open to minimize the sound of her breath. But there was nothing, so she returned to the pages.

Another noise, this time louder. And closer. Layna twitched. She closed the manuscript and crawled off the bed, knocking over a stuffed bear with a graduation cap. Something from a friend on the mainland, though she couldn't remember exactly who had given it to her. At least not right at that moment.

Her feet hit the carpeted floor, and she shuffled to the door.

She pressed the side of her face against it, and waited.

Still, she heard nothing.

With one hand flat on the door, she unlocked the deadbolt, then pulled the door open just enough to see outside. Her foot wedged against it at the bottom, just in case.

Warm light from the hallway etched its way vertically down her face and body. When Layna heard and saw nothing, she slid her foot away and opened the door wider.

She stepped into the hallway. She was alone. The streamers on the door across the hall from her were still, so the stairwell door must not have been opened. She slid across the hall and checked that door. Locked. Her hand grazed the wall as she walked down the corridor and checked every door she passed. Locked, locked, locked. And then she reached the stairwell door.

Layna looked through its long glass window. She saw nothing when she looked left, then right. She turned back to the hallway behind her, and suddenly the hairs on the back of her neck raised. There was nobody, of course, and she knew it. She turned back to the stairwell door, ready to leave.

Then she screamed.

Max's face popped into view through the glass. Layna jumped back, her instincts telling her to run.

Max entered the hallway, followed by Nancy.

"Jesus Christ, Max!" Layna yelled, hitting him on the shoulder.

"Ow, babe, I'm sorry," Max said. "We didn't mean to scare you. What are you doing alone, anyway?"

"What are you two doing skulking around campus?"

Max and Nancy looked at one another, but neither offered an answer.

Layna continued. "I've been reading that thing my mother wrote. Guys, it's weird. It's scaring me. I really think we're in trouble."

Nancy finally spoke. "You don't know the half of it."

Layna looked at her quizzically as Max took her hand.

"Grab it and let's go," he said.

The rain continued to fall as Layna, Max, and Nancy left the dorm and made their way across the campus. Layna had her book bag slung over a shoulder. Inside was the play, tucked away.

"I don't understand all of it," Layna said, "but it kinda reads like some sort of revenge treatise."

"How Unabomber of your mother," Nancy said with a straight face.

Layna ignored the comment, but Max gave a *Really?* glance at Nancy, who shrugged it off.

Layna went on. "The lead character is after someone for something they did to her."

"What was it?" Max asked.

"I don't know. The last act of the play is missing."

"What did Crosby think?" Nancy wondered.

Layna shrugged. "He didn't stay. I told him I was going to read it and he seemed—I don't know." But she did know. Or, at least felt she did.

"Upset?" Nancy chimed in.

The words bit Layna. She didn't want to deal with it. Not then. Not ever. "I have every right to choose what I wanna work on, and this is so much bigger than that. How could you, or he, anyone, think the showcase matters now?"

"I'm sorry, you're right," Nancy said, grimacing. "He's just been distant."

"Where is he now?" Max asked.

"He said he was going to see if he could dig anything else up about the play, or my mother," Layna said. "Frankly, I never did much digging at all. I've seen a few photos of me as a baby, a few of her, and the clipping about her car accident."

"I don't wanna sound like a jerk," Nancy stated, "but you probably wouldn't have gotten too far, since you only just now found out you have a new last name. Or a real one. Or something."

"The fun part of learning your life is a lie," Layna said sadly. It might have been the first real truth since all of the drama surrounding them, surrounding Layna, started.

"If Nancy and I have been together, and Crosby was with you, who does that leave?" Max wondered.

"Alice," Nancy said.

Layna put her hand in her bag and felt the pages of the play. "Dillon," she said, though she hated to admit it. "I don't know where he's been or what he's up to."

"That's a first," Max said.

Layna was too tired to fight again, so she kept her mouth shut. She brushed a thick clump of wet hair from her face, and she saw Nancy and Max's eyes widen.

"Oh my God. Layn, you're bleeding!" Nancy said.

Layna stared at her hand. Thin streams of red snaked through her fingers as raindrops hit them. She wiped her forehead again and looked down. There was less blood, but it was blood nonetheless.

"It's not me! I don't understand. It's not me," Layna repeated.

"It's your bag," Max revealed, pointing at it.

All three of them stared down.

Layna was stunned, worried. Her bag was tinged in the bottom corner with red. She dropped it to the ground.

Max grabbed it and opened it. "Oh, God."

"What is it?" Layna demanded.

Max pulled something dark and wet from the bag.

"What the hell is that?" Nancy asked.

Crimson streamed from his fingers as he held it in his open palm. A severed rabbit's foot. A real one, Layna knew, cut harshly with something rough. Prickles of bone jutted out from its end.

It sickened her. But what scared her, and Max and Nancy as well, was the note. It was typed, its message simple:

you'll need this

"Is this a joke?" Layna asked, though she knew it wasn't.

"It's a warning," Max offered. He threw it back into Layna's bag. "Now do you believe me? Something happened to Alice. And if we don't do something about it, I think we're next."

Layna felt lightheaded. First Sydney killed herself, though Layna questioned that theory. And then Alice went missing, or worse. And now a warning.

"We need help," Nancy said. "We need to find Daniel. And that detective."

"And Dillon," Max spat out. "I wanna know what he's been up to."

For the first time on that subject, Layna agreed with Max. She had hoped Max was wrong about Dillon. But now, she didn't know.

The three friends walked into the night toward the security building.

Layna turned back and squinted through the rain and darkness. She thought she saw movement, maybe a person. Or, she thought, more likely it was her imagination.

But her mind hadn't played a trick on her. They were being watched.

And Layna did not know that it was Dillon watching, and when he lurched forward from behind a tree, when he flinched at a crackle of thunder, when something solid hit him on the back of the head, Layna did not see the boy she had once almost loved as he crumpled to the ground at the feet of the killer.

CHAPTER XII

The green glow of a photocopier in motion sliced across its glass bed. The slit of light hit Crosby's waist as he stood over it and waited. The copy spit out the side, but Crosby took no notice. He stared off into the distance toward the archives building.

It wasn't so long ago that he and Layna discovered the secret the school was keeping. Not so long ago they bumped into Dillon and Mrs. D'Arcangelo, and wondered why they were together. And it was not so long ago that he was sitting in Layna's room trying to find the words to ask her if she would consider using something he had written for her showcase. To help him shine in his senior year, when he might not have had the chance otherwise. He had barely started the conversation when Layna shot him down.

Crosby sighed and resigned himself to the thought that it wasn't fair. But neither was it fair that Layna had been thrust into everything the way she had. He suddenly wondered, and was not sure why, if he was the only one who thought of Sydney's death in the thick of all the madness. That, somehow, it was a catalyst. He had to wonder how it looked to those around him, how much he worried not about the pain, the shattered glass, and the blood of Sydney's fall, but his own trajectory after the event. Maybe he cared less than he wanted to believe he did, or less than he wanted others to think he did. All of these thoughts bore down on and upset him. The school, the deaths, and Alice missing. It all made him wish he had left the island. Overbearing parents would be welcome right about now.

He wiped his shiny face with his hands and ran his fingers through his hair. He pulled the piece of paper from the output tray and studied the words from the newspaper headline. Phrases leapt out at him.

"Fire."

"Foul Play."

"Student death."

They each hit him hard. He looked up, trying not to think *history repeats itself.*

He grabbed the paper and put it with others he had already researched. He stuffed them into his backpack, clicked off the copier, and left the original on its bed. He moved toward the door. His shadows grew longer and shorter as he passed the overhead lights.

As he left the building, the storm had let up enough so that he could see patches of starry night, but the air was still heavy with moisture he could feel on his skin as he made his way back to Layna's.

As he neared the black box theater, something in the periphery of his vision pulled his attention. It was small, and it fumbled around on the wet grass.

Two white rabbits. His white rabbits.

"No. No, no, no," he said as he ran to them. He grabbed them and cradled them in his arms. "How did you two get out?"

The answer became clear as Crosby entered the theater, went backstage, and flipped on the lights. Everything he had worked to create for his magic act was in a state of utter disarray. Props were strewn about, and the rabbit cages' doors were torn from their hinges like they had been pried off with a hammer.

Crosby surveyed the scene and couldn't believe it. Who would do this? Why? He put the rabbits back in their cages and jury-rigged a door by placing the backs of two chairs against them. It would work for the time being.

As he shuffled through the space, he heard a noise. A whimper?

Somebody else was in the building.

Crosby stepped past the thick black fly curtains that separated the backstage from the front, past the dim ghost lamp, and clicked on the main lights. He barely had time to register what he saw.

"Jesus!" Crosby ran to Dillon, shocked to see him gagged, bound with rope around his wrists and ankles, and strapped to a bed of nails.

Detective Parker sat alone at the security desk. He looked at the clock and saw that it was later than he had thought. Although the storm had started to subside, thunder still crackled in the distance. Parker was reminded of being a child, counting the seconds between the lightning and the thunder. The lower the number, the closer the storm. He never paid attention to how true it was. When you're a small boy, no amount of counting calmed the fear of shattering thunder.

Storms always forced him to remember the night he found out his parents had died in a fire. It was hard for him to understand then how the two people who raised him for six years could have perished in a fire when it had been raining so hard. His mother's sister was babysitting when the call had come. He knew something was wrong when she started crying and dropped the phone, covering her mouth with both hands and wailing. It was the kind of crying that looked like it hurt. And it hurt him to see it. Tears welled in his eyes, even though he had no idea what was going on. That all changed when she sat him down, tears still dripping down her face, to explain that the building his parents were in for their office party had caught fire. He was sure there was more, but it had all started to merge with a ringing in his ear, and though his aunt continued to move her lips, he had no idea what she said.

At the funeral, and for years and years to come, Parker would learn more of the details: the electrical fire started in a break room, the curtains went up, a gas line ruptured and exploded, the building rocked, and trapped people burnt to death in the disaster. A party to celebrate a merger between two companies saw its joy blown away like ashes in the wind.

He never felt the same afterward, never felt whole. It was something the big man worked at but could never truly control. There was nothing to do now. The past was the past.

Parker was startled from his memories when the door to the security office opened, letting in a gust of damp air. Following in its wake were Layna, Max, and Nancy.

"What happened to your face?" Parker blurted out when he saw the red across Layna's forehead. He stood up.

She shook her head. "It's—forget it, it's not mine."

Parker regarded her warily as Nancy stepped up. "Where's Daniel?" she asked.

"Good question," Max shot back. Daniel's whereabouts were something the three of them had never considered.

"He went to check on the phones," Parker said. "They're out."

"Shocker," Max offered. He grabbed Layna's bloody bag and threw it on the security guard's desk. It flopped open, and Parker cocked his head to see the severed rabbit's foot and the note.

"Don't strain," Nancy said, seeing Parker squint to read the note. "We'll save you the time. It's part of a dead animal, and it's pretty clear it was no accident."

Parker looked up at her, then at Layna. He remained calm and tried to speak in a manner that would put the kids at ease. "What

I see here might very well be a prank—"

"Are you kidding me?" Layna yelled out, incredulous.

Parker didn't skip a beat. "—being pulled on all of you. On top of your friend being missing, which we are doing our best to—"

Max slammed his hands down on the desk. "Dammit, Alice is not missing. She's dead! Can't you get that through your thick skull?"

"I need you to calm down," Parker said, his voice exuding authority. "Let me help you all figure this out."

Max huffed and turned away from the desk. Parker pulled out his walkie-talkie, clicked the button, and spoke into it after the dead air squelch subsided. "Daniel, I have some of your kids in the office. What's your twenty?"

No one spoke as they waited for a response. Max looked at Parker, who looked at Layna, who looked at Nancy. The round robin of worry and wonder broke when the radio came to life.

"Done with the phones," Daniel's voice said through static. "It's beyond me. I'm checking the perimeter and then on my way back. Over."

Parker lifted the walkie up with a slight grimace, as if to let the kids know, *Stop worrying*. It had little effect on them. Layna threw something else on the desk. Parker watched it slide toward him.

The manuscript. The play by Amanda Kincaid.

"Alice found this," Layna stated without raising her voice. "Now she's gone. The phones are out. And now there's part of a dead rabbit in my bag with a note that pretty much screams *you're going to die*."

Parker picked up the manuscript and thumbed through its old, dirty pages.

"This play used superstitions to explore the prejudice and hate of a community. This community. This *school*," Layna added. "My mother wrote this because they shunned her for something she did."

Parker rubbed his brow. "I'm sorry about what might have happened back then. And I'm sorry you had to find out like this—"

"That's not what I'm saying!" Layna exploded. "The superstitions in this play were used to kill people. This play was about *murder*. Are you listening? Do you understand? It reads like a damn blueprint for what's going on here."

Parker wasn't sure what to say, and he could see the others felt the same. He watched as Layna paid him no attention, instead flipping wildly through the pages.

"You think I'm crazy. Listen to this. The first death deals with an umbrella being opened indoors," Layna said, before reading directly from the play. "'Gut wrenching agony, from which no umbrella could provide me shelter.'"

Parker watched her, waiting for more. He didn't want to appear uncaring, but he wanted to know what she was getting at. "And?"

"And? And then a girl is thrown out a goddamn window!" Layna yelled.

Parker could not ignore the fact that hearing this stirred their feelings of fear and worry. He knew they, especially Max, might not handle things appropriately if Parker didn't find a way to treat the situation rationally. The only way to do that, he thought, was to tell the truth. Or at least a part of it.

"I'm listening. I'm hearing you. And it concerns me," he told them. "I will tell you there was an open umbrella in the room of the young girl who jumped."

His plan did not work. Layna looked ready to pounce. He could see it in her eyes as they tightened. In her face as she grimaced.

"Jumped? Are you even listening to me?" Layna asked.

Max chimed in. "What are we gonna do? What are *you* gonna

do about all this?"

Nancy had had enough of the yelling, and the theories, and the accusations about who was or wasn't doing something. "Guys, please stop," she said. "Layn, if that thing is what you say it is, then what happens next?"

Layna looked down at the manuscript. Parker could tell she did not want to say it.

"Something with a black cat," Layna offered.

Parker opened the drawer of the desk and pulled out Alice's now black keychain. He watched the reactions of each of the kids, and he knew that they knew something terrible had started on the island the night Sydney died.

That it was continuing with Alice.

And that they were, most likely, next.

The knots were tight.

Crosby stared at Dillon's angry pink, squirming hands. He worked his short-nailed fingers around and over the taut bindings, though it did nothing but make Dillon panic in muffled grunts.

"I can't get this! I need a knife. Who did this to you?" Crosby wondered as he looked upward, momentarily blinded by the glaring stage lights shining down on them.

A bubble of snot leaked out of Dillon's nose as he tried to scream through the duct tape. Looking at him, so helpless, Crosby wondered how he had ever thought he'd call Dillon a friend. Even so, he was not one to watch anyone suffer, so he reached forward as Dillon continued to thrash.

"Dude, stop. I'm trying," Crosby yelled. It did nothing to make Dillon quit bugging his eyes, cease his useless yelling, or end his head thrusting.

Then Crosby had a sudden moment of clarity. He ripped the tape to reveal a ball of fabric lodged in Dillon's mouth.

"Behind you!" Dillon cried out. Crosby heard the words, but they didn't register. And then they did.

Standing behind Crosby was the killer, ready to strike. The boy's instincts took over as he crouched down low, turned around, and yanked on the killer's left leg with all of his power. The killer went down with a hard thud, but not before the knife in his hand scraped Crosby's arm.

Crosby saw the wound before he felt it, and even then, there was little pain. It was the warm flow of blood running down his skin that caused his body to pump adrenaline.

Dillon was saying something, screaming, but the sounds disappeared into a muffled cacophony inside Crosby's head. He focused on getting out, staying alive, getting help. *I'm not gonna die here*, he thought.

He leapt to his feet and ran for the theater doors. His screams broke the barrier his body had put up to compartmentalize what was going on. He could hear everything around him once again, mainly Dillon's screams.

Arms outstretched, Crosby ran for the doors, slamming into them. They opened only enough for his hands and forearms to burst in pain from the force of his momentum. He went down, bouncing off the doors that were chained from the other side.

"Dammit!" he screamed as he got to his feet, more slowly. "Help me! Somebody!" He pushed and pushed against the doors as he yelled, though he knew it was no use. He squeezed his face through the scant opening, hoping it would amplify his call. When he turned his head back to see what was happening behind him, his view was met with an arc of gleaming silver.

For a second Crosby believed he saw a spark when he pulled

his head back and the metal blade raked against the metal door. When the killer stalled for a split second, Crosby balled his bloody, bruised hand into a fist and rammed it into the gut of his attacker. A muted cough came from behind the mask as the assailant doubled over.

Crosby took his chance to run.

He wasn't sure where he would run, but he had little time to think before the attacker's black boot caught between his own legs. Crosby went down. His face slammed into the back of one of the theater's wooden seats. This time he immediately felt the pain of teeth knocked loose, a broken nose, and what would be a swollen eye. Blood filled his mouth. He groaned as he lay face down on the dirty carpet. The pain grew, then he was flipped over on his back.

Tears clouded Crosby's vision as the killer stood over him. All he could think was who might be under the mask.

"No," Crosby tried to utter, spitting a tooth out even as his tongue ran over the pulpy root of another one already gone. The evil mask both grinned and frowned, growing bigger as it creeped closer and closer to Crosby's own face.

One of the last things he thought about was Dillon.

How terrible it was to have run away from him.

How they were never friends. Not really.

How he could have tried harder.

How he left him there to die.

And how it was now his turn.

CHAPTER XIV

"There's no way off the island until Monday," Daniel said to Max, after returning from checking the perimeter. He shook off his hat, which was slick with moisture. "What we need to do—"

"Listen, asshat," Max exploded. He picked up the manuscript splayed out on the table. The thing that had caused so much trouble, so much pain. So many secrets.

"You don't get it, neither of you," he added, looking from Daniel to Parker and back again. "It's all right here in these pages. What's going to happen, how it's going to happen. The messed up thing is we still don't know why, and I blame McKenna for that. If you two don't do something to get us off this rock, one by one, we are going to die."

Max looked at Layna, whose eyes roamed across everyone in the room. He knew she was thinking exactly what he was.

Who would be next? Who was doing this?

Max also wondered who was going to help them, if not Daniel or Parker.

Nancy grabbed the script from Max's hands. "Jesus Christ, if you're all gonna sit there and act like Helen Keller, I'll figure it out."

"What I'd like everyone to do is calm down," Parker said calmly. "We'll find everyone, stay together, and we will get off the island safely."

"You did a bang-up job with Alice," Max said. "If you had listened to me—" But he stopped himself. More to the point, the lump in his throat stopped him.

Layna grabbed his hand and locked her fingers with his, turning toward Nancy as she flipped through the script. "Well?"

Nancy stopped turning pages and slowly ran her finger across the lines of black ink. "It isn't specific," Nancy offered, "but this is what it says."

Parker stood. "Before anybody starts jumping to conclusions, let's remember this is a piece of fiction."

Max shook his head in disbelief, even as he watched Daniel nod his. "It's a piece of fiction somebody wants to turn into a really cuckootown crazypants version of MTV's *True Life*," he stated. "Maybe, 'I Was a Teenaged Murder Victim?' So, I'm all ears, Nancy. Go ahead."

Parker cocked his head and Max felt the man was unhappy with the attitude he was throwing. But Max didn't care. And he didn't like the detective.

Nancy read, "Should the white hare cross the wayfarer's path from right to left, his journey will be disastrous." When she was done she realized the room was silent.

It was Daniel who broke the stillness. "I thought a rabbit, at least the rabbit's foot, was lucky."

It sickened Max he hadn't thought of it before. That his friend, their friend, was out there alone, maybe hurt, maybe worse, and here they were, locked away safe and warm and talking about their fate in a way that felt strangely, frighteningly cavalier.

He turned to Nancy and frowned. He knew she would be affected the most. "White rabbits?" he asked.

"Oh, God," Nancy yelped, dropping the script. "Crosby's next!"

The grating sound of thick metal chain against the smooth metal door rang through the lobby of the black box theater. Layna covered her ears. Daniel yanked as hard as he could to open it, but the padlock prevented any real give. Great lengths, she thought, were taken by someone to make sure there was no escape.

"Dammit!" Daniel cried out.

"Do something, help him!" Nancy added. Tears streamed down her face.

Layna thought they matched her own.

"Jesus!" Max said, pushing past Daniel and Parker.

Layna could not make out what was in his hand. Then the silver edge of a sharpened axe crashed down on the chain. She let out a yelp and grabbed Nancy as Max brought the blade down again and again.

"Ow!" he yelped when the axe hit the door and snapped back in his hands. He dropped the axe and shook them.

Parker grabbed the wooden handle, raised it over his head, and slammed it down in exactly the right spot.

Layna let out a breath when she saw the chain snap in two. The detective threw the axe to the ground and, with his big hands, pulled the metal links from their snakelike hold on the door handles.

Nancy tried to barge in the theater, but Daniel held her back.

"Crosby, we're coming!" she bellowed.

But they weren't coming. Not all of them. In fact, Layna was glad Daniel and Parker disappeared into the theater. She didn't want Max to go in at all. And though she assumed Crosby was inside, hurt, or worse, she didn't want to go in, either.

With the doors fully open, she and Max had a full view. She saw his head droop, and she swore she saw another tear. She had now seen Max cry more in the last few days than she had in the last few years.

Layna didn't stop Nancy as she ran to the doors, screaming at the top of her lungs, "*No, no, no!*" Her high-pitched echo rang through the building and shot through Layna.

Layna took a step forward, and then another. Max tried to stop her. Nancy crumpled to the ground, weeping and screaming. Layna watched as her friend's shoulders heaved up and down, and when Nancy looked up at her, Layna felt as if she didn't know the girl.

Layna pushed into the theater. She had not wanted to see, but now, strangely, all she wanted was to see.

And there, the middle of the theater, was Crosby.

Bound in thick rope soaked red. Hanging upside down. His insides on the outside.

Layna turned to the side and retched the little food she had in her belly. She heard Parker tell Daniel to get her and the others out of there. She heard Nancy's blubbering screams and unintelligible babble. She heard Max's swearing.

As Daniel ushered them from the theater, she thought she heard something else. In the distance. Another cry, but not Nancy's. Another voice, but not Max's. She wrenched herself free and turned back toward the aisle.

"Layna, stop," Parker demanded from the doorway. And she did.

Layna pointed to the stage, at something no one had noticed among the gore of Crosby's corpse.

Dillon. He was covered in blood. He tried to cry out, but all that came was a whimper.

JINXED

Everyone was tense inside the small, sterile clinic. The colorless walls were filled with garish posters about the dangers of not being vaccinated, the perils of drinking alcohol, and, God forbid, teen pregnancy. Layna could not have felt worse.

D'Arcangelo and McKenna had arrived, which made Layna's stomach flip and flop. She grabbed Max's arm and held it tightly, watching as D'Arcangelo tried to comfort Nancy, who had stopped sobbing and now stared blankly. McKenna said and did nothing. Layna hated him even more for that.

Daniel tended to Dillon. He was covered in dirt and blood, but the wounds weren't life-threatening. High school wasn't supposed to be life-threatening, Layna thought. Dillon grimaced as Daniel cleaned a gash on his arm, finally wrapping it in gauze.

When he was done, Daniel wiped his sweaty forehead with the back of a rubber-gloved hand. "That's it. That's all I can do here," he said.

Parker stood. "This is insane. Where's the nurse? *Is* there a nurse?"

McKenna stood too, but he failed to match Parker. There was no match, Layna thought. One was strapping, the other old. One was concerned, the other a politician.

"I beg your pardon, Detective, but I can assure you none of this was planned," McKenna said.

"You have absolutely no idea what is truly going on here, do you?" Parker asked, loud enough for everyone to hear. "This place, all the secrets it harbors, all the lies you have kept locked away, have done nothing but fester. And now here we are, in the middle of an explosion of truth that has led to murder. For a long time people have wondered about this island, this school. And even you, Harlan. But when all of this is over, they will know, and you will have to answer to them. Coming clean is the one thing that scares you more than losing donors, isn't it? More than losing precious tuition when a student drops out? Maybe even more than murder."

"How dare you?" McKenna hissed.

Layna, like the others, watched the exchange as if it were the beginning of a heated tennis match. She readied for the back and forth, one that teetered on a precipice where the options were life and death.

McKenna stepped up to Parker. He was smaller than the detective, but there was something grander about the older man, Layna thought. Something that cloaked the man from the harm of his own or others' words and deeds.

"This is not just a *place.*" McKenna quietly spit with an erudite demeanor to rival Miranda Priestly in *The Devil Wears Prada*. The ridiculous idea made Layna smile, at least on the inside, as she imagined a montage of McKenna throwing fur coats on his assistant's desk.

"This is getting us nowhere," D'Arcangelo said. "The fact is, we don't have the resources we need right now."

Layna didn't care what McKenna thought of her, or any of them. "Arguing about it won't bring them any closer," she said.

"Unacceptable," Parker said. "We have got to reach the mainland and get everyone off the island."

"I do not disagree," McKenna stated coolly. "But the fact remains that we have no way of contacting them."

Layna was sickened by his carefree hand-waving and readied to speak when Parker's fist flew down on the desk in front of him. It startled everyone. Papers blew to the side and floated to the floor.

"We are talking about murder!" he screamed.

Layna flinched at the force of his words. They were scary. He was scary.

"I can understand no cell reception," Parker went on. "What about getting online? We can—"

"It's out," Nancy said. "I already tried. We're, like, literally on prototype Internet here. Nice *place*." She threw the pointed last words at McKenna.

"And the phones are out?" Parker asked.

Daniel nodded.

D'Arcangelo met the dean's quizzical stare. Layna immediately wondered what weren't they telling her. Or any of them.

"Goddamit," Parker cursed, pacing. "Are you telling me there's no way to get a message off this rock?" He stopped and turned, stiffly glaring at McKenna and D'Arcangelo. "What have you done?"

"There's a CB radio," Max offered.

"Yes, there is, as a matter of fact," McKenna said. "I assume you are familiar with it after breaking into my cottage."

"Sorry not sorry," Max offered without a hint of remorse. "Sue me. Arrest me. Do whatever you want if it will get me out of here and as far away from you and your craptastic school as possible."

Layna grabbed Max's hand. She needed him to be stable for her.

"Jesus Christ," Nancy said, directly at McKenna, "you're the master of this whole operation and you sound dodgier than a newbie. Max knew about your precious radio in your precious cottage because we were trying to call for help when you were nowhere to be found."

"Why didn't you use it to call the mainland?" Parker asked.

Layna also desperately wanted to know. She looked around as if the answer was going to flutter down from the rafters above.

"Max?" Layna asked.

"Because someone smashed it to bits before we got there." Max said it like an accusation. "Like they knew we needed to use it. But you, Dean, already knew that, didn't you? You always know."

Layna had had more than enough bickering. She wanted answers. Needed a plan. "Forget the radio. Don't you see? It's all laid out. Somebody is on this campus, murdering us one by one. And they're using this play as their roadmap."

D'Arcangelo stepped toward Layna, but the girl backed away. She did not want to be touched, bothered, mothered by her. Not now. Not like this.

"And you knew. You knew all along," she said to the teacher, her mentor and confidant. She then turned back to McKenna. "Why didn't you tell me my mother went to school here? Is my scholarship hush money? What else are you hiding from me?"

"This is preposterous!" McKenna said.

"Yeah, not so much," Max said.

McKenna looked angrier than Layna had ever seen him. He stepped toward Max. "You watch your tongue, young man, or—"

"Or you'll what?" Max wondered. "People. Are. *Dying*! It has something to do with this place. This play. *You*!"

A small voice came from the back. "Me."

Everyone turned. It was Dillon. Layna had almost forgot he was there. Dirty, bloody Dillon.

"Why didn't he kill me?" Dillon whispered. He was met with silence. "I was tied up, but he didn't kill me. I was bait to lure Crosby. Oh, God, now he's—"

He stopped himself, and though nobody rushed to comfort him or refute the idea, Layna could see the very notion he put forth haunted Nancy.

"We're all targets," Parker said.

Nancy went toward the door. "Me? Why would anybody wanna kill me?" She turned to Dillon. "But, I'll give you an A-plus on your theory. Maybe you were supposed to die. And just maybe Crosby was at the wrong place at the wrong time. And you should be dead and he should be alive."

"Nancy, stop!" Layna said.

Nancy turned on Layna. "You, too. You and your family and your mother and your scholarship and that damned play. You could have done something about it."

"I didn't know," Layna said, hurt.

"That's not fair," Max said as he sidled up to Layna.

"Not—not *fair*?" Nancy screamed. "Crosby was murdered because nobody did anything about it. And now we're all either a suspect or a victim? Screw this. Screw you." She raised her hands and both middle fingers. "All of you."

She left the door open as they watched her disappear into the night.

"Dammit," Parker said, turning to Daniel. "Go watch her."

Daniel did, not bothering to close the door. Wind brought a chill into the already icy room.

"I'm sorry to say, Dean," Parker said, "but it looks like your school, and your precious showcase, are closed." McKenna looked like he had been run through with a spear. "The rest of you, stay together," Parker continued. "Go back to the security office, lock the door, and wait."

Layna and Max led the way out. Dillon followed.

When they were outside, Layna heard the deadbolt of the nurse's office latch. She pulled Max to stop him and raised a finger to Dillon to keep him quiet. She pressed her ear against the door to listen.

But she could only make out Parker.

"This has gone on long enough. It's time for the both of you to talk."

CHAPTER XV

Max gripped Layna's hand as they went down the stairs of the clinic. He knew he might be holding on a little too tight, or pulling too hard, but he wanted to get them both out of there. He wanted to forget everything that had happened and everything that had been said. The easiest way to do that was to find a safe place to hide. The illusion, and he knew it was an illusion, was shattered when he heard a deep voice from behind them.

"Max, Layna, wait." Dillon. Trying to keep up in his bandaged, bruised state.

Max didn't want to wait, but Layna stopped him. His lips tightened and he huffed out a breath, angry. He knew Layna could sense it, but he didn't care. He took his hand from hers and turned to face Dillon.

"I am not going anywhere with you," Max proclaimed. "Sorry, bud, you're so on your own."

"We can't do that. Not now," Layna said. "You heard Parker. We stick together. And he's hurt."

Max shut Dillon out of his mind, shut the campus, the world, the death, out of his mind. He took Layna by the shoulders and bore his brown eyes into her blue ones. Even now, wet, tired, and afraid, he saw she was beautiful. It centered him. "You and I are the only 'we' I care about, all right? I cannot let anything happen to you."

Layna visibly relaxed. Max knew she was torn, but he was

right. At this point he wasn't concerned about the feelings of her ex-boyfriend, who seemed to cause trouble whenever he showed up. Maybe he *was* bait. Maybe he should have been more. It was an awful thing to think, and Max felt bad as the thought struck him, but what else was there to think?

He nudged Layna to the side and struck a sad, hushed tone as he spoke to Dillon. "As far as I'm concerned, this piece of trash can make it on his own. He survived once. It must be his lucky day."

"How do I know it wasn't you under that mask in the theater?" Dillon responded.

"Don't say that," Layna said.

Max could hear the hurt in her voice, found the very idea of the not-so-thinly veiled threat laughable, and he knew Dillon knew it. He stepped up to his rival calmly. He was sick of yelling. Loud or not, the message would be the same, and he wanted Dillon not only to hear it, but to feel it. "Because, bitch, if it was me, you wouldn't be standing here right now." He spat on the ground at Dillon's feet and turned to Layna. "Let's go. Just us."

Max was glad when Layna did not turn back to look at Dillon. But when he turned back, Max saw, through the clinic window, Parker, D'Arcangelo, and McKenna in a heated argument. Parker turned, saw Max, and slowly closed the blinds.

Nancy ran as fast as she could into the dance building. She pulled the door shut and leaned against it. She was no longer crying. It seemed futile to do so. Her face, she imagined, looked a mess. She'd find out soon enough inside the studio. As her instructors had told her all her life, the mirrors never lie.

She stood in the dark for a few moments, catching her breath and wondering where Max and Layna had gone, then figured they would have been the ones, at least Layna would, to listen to the adults and go to the safety of the security office.

Nancy chuckled at the idea of safety. Here they were on an island usually full of students dancing, singing, and acting, but they had been reduced to a handful of people running, screaming, and dying. She hated to think it all seemed like a movie, like something that happens to other people, real or not. But it was really happening to them. The thought made her recognize she had done everything she should not have done: yelled at her friends, ran off hysterical into the night, and now she was alone. In the dark.

She clicked the lights on and felt a fraction safer as the fluorescents came to life with a soft tinkle. She was never a fan of how they made her look, but right now, off-putting shadows and garish color on her face, were the least of her concerns. She'd meet up with the others soon. But for now, she needed to be alone. To think of what to do, to think of Crosby, to think of herself.

Dancing helped. It wasn't just something Nancy did, or was good at. She felt she simply *was* dancing. For as long as she could remember. The frilly clothes, the overdone makeup, the competition. There was nothing about it she didn't love. And she really felt she was good.

Now, though, faced with her own mortality, she wondered if she'd ever make it in the real world. Would she be a star, a working dancer, or the guy from the movie *Fame* who set out to make his dreams come true and then came back to New York to wait tables when it all crashed and burned?

She hated asking herself those questions. Why couldn't she just enjoy the dance? Would it ever matter? What if someone did want to kill her? She tried to push aside these paralyzing thoughts.

Yet here she was. They all were. And right then she missed Layna, told herself she was sorry, hoping her friend could feel it.

And as she turned the corner and faced the double doors of the studio, Nancy felt something else. She rolled her eyes.

"I know you're there watching me," she called out. "And it's creepy. And I'm fine. As fine as I can be, considering that my name is apparently on the chopping block." She leaned her head back around the corner and saw Daniel near the doors.

The security guard stepped forward. "Detective Parker wanted me to make sure you were all right. I didn't mean to scare you."

"You didn't scare me," Nancy said, and she meant it. "Unless you're the killer, in which case, well, I'm still not so sure I'd be afraid. Sorry." She meant that, too, and watched Daniel's smile fade.

"Me? No. No! I'm not, why would I—"

"Danny boy, I know. It was a joke," Nancy offered. "Just try, you know, to amp down the creepy 'watching me' factor by, like, all of it, okay?"

Daniel saluted her, then looked nervously at his hand.

"We're all doomed," she said as she headed into the mirrored studio.

Daniel watched as Nancy slinked into the studio. As the door closed, the lights in the hallway shut off. He assumed she turned them off by accident.

"Hey, the lights!" he said.

He heard, and felt, the thump of music starting up. He was moving slowly against the wall to find the light switch when he thought he heard something else. He stopped, staying as still as he could.

Breathing. He heard breathing. It must be his own, he

thought. He sucked in air and held it. There was no sound except for the dance beats. Still he held the air in his lungs, which started to burn, to feel tight. Still nothing. He was about to release the air when he heard someone else do it first.

Daniel didn't have time to scream—didn't think to scream—when he saw the man who stood next to him. He saw the mask, which grinned and frowned.

"Hey!" was all he got out before being grabbed and spun around. An arm went around his throat and stopped his scream. His muffled, choked gurgles mixed with the sound of his vinyl jacket as it rubbed against the coarse, dark fabric the killer wore.

Daniel tried to gain some sort of upper hand, but it was futile. He felt the killer's grip, not much more powerful than his, but he couldn't get any leverage. He flailed his arms, panicking, and his eyes glazed over as stars filled his vision.

But Daniel told himself not to give in or give up. He mustered the fight left in him and kicked out as hard and fast as he could, but all it did was knock over a metal folding chair, which slid from the wall to the ground and reverberated like a saucer spinning to silence on a counter.

Daniel started to cry. And he hated it.

Then gleaming, silver flashes bouncing moonlight swept toward him between his muffled cries, and a blade raked deeply across his throat, severing the carotid arteries. Blood poured forth from between the useless fingers he held against the wound. His eyes went wide as he understood that it was a gaping hole, large enough for his fingers to slide into as he tried to stop the bleeding.

No air came out with the final scream Daniel tried to force. With his hand literally reaching inside his own neck, he started to pass out, taking a stack of the metal chairs down with him. He felt the warmth of blood and the cool linoleum beneath him.

The last thing Daniel saw was the killer stepping over him as if he were a sleeping child.

If only, Daniel managed to think before he died in a puddle of himself.

Nancy's leg was in full stretch at the bar when she heard a loud noise beyond the studio doors that worried her. She stopped swaying to the deep bass rhythm and yelled to Daniel. "I told you. Creepy."

The resulting silence both assuaged and worried her. Daniel was there to make sure she was all right, but a pang of doubt hit the pit of her stomach. She hoped he was all right.

She heard chairs hitting the floor, and it did not sit well with her. She pulled her leg from atop the bar and inched toward the door. Maybe whatever just happened in the hallway was a mix-up. Or Daniel just left. Or it was the wind. But she knew better.

She reached the door, grasped the handles, and pulled hard. She wasn't going to tiptoe. Energy coursed through her as if she had just competed and won at competition. But this was no competition, she reminded herself. This was survival. And now she was going to make sure Daniel was all right. Role-reversal, she thought. She had always had a soft spot in her heart for Danny boy.

Nancy hadn't expected the hallway to be dark. "Danny?" she yelled. No one responded, so she reached for the light and flipped it on. Nothing. Off and on. Nothing. Third time is the charm, she thought, but it wasn't.

"Damn," she said. There was no sound except distant thunder. The storm was passing. She didn't lie to herself. She hated this. She was scared. She wanted her cell phone, wanted it to work. But nothing she wanted was going to happen. This place had become a horror movie. She acknowledged that she committed a cardinal sin when she left the group. She tried to push aside the silly thought that just because splitting up worked in Scooby-Doo didn't mean it was going to work for her.

Nancy shook off the cartoon thoughts. She turned the corner of the darkened hallway and was relieved to see Daniel sitting in a chair. His back was to her, his head was cocked to one side, and the chair sat in the middle of the hallway, blocking the door. She felt relieved that he was manning the door, but oddly, there were no chairs on the floor, collapsed at odd angles. They were neatly stacked against the wall. What had she heard?

She approached Daniel, glad she was no longer alone. "Don't take this the wrong way, like I'm down to Netflix and chill, but thank God you're here. I'd seriously rather have you sneaking a peek than—"

Then she saw blood on the floor. A vengeful crimson puddle at Daniel's feet. She followed it up from his pants to the front of his jacket, where it melded with the dark fabric and had made its way from the man's slit throat.

The angry wound beckoned to her with a meaty, saw-toothed grin.

Nancy screamed. Deep, guttural, primal. A noise of one who knows death is not just near, but imminent. Her frozen muscles seemed to thaw, and she pushed past Daniel's dead body as he slumped forward and fell to her feet. She leapt over him, reached the doors to the outside, and was about to push when a face suddenly sprang into view and shook her to the core. It dared to taunt with two opposite emotions as it stared at her—into her. Predator and prey. Lightning flashed, illuminating the mask, but not the sunken black eye holes that belonged to the man who wanted to kill her.

Nancy turned back toward the studio and ran, not thinking about the red sheet of blood on the floor. She slipped, but did not fall, grabbing the chairs stacked against the wall. She regained her balance as they crashed to the floor and spilled in front of the door the killer had just opened, making it difficult to open it all the way. Not impossible, but enough to give her a chance to get away even as she saw the blade in the killer's left hand swipe in a wide arc.

She ran along the darkened hallway to the dance studio. Flying inside, she slammed the doors behind her and locked them. She took a moment to catch her breath and assess her options. But the respite was short-lived. She flew forward and a yelp escaped her lips as the doors she leaned against were pounded on from the other side. Nancy covered her mouth as she saw the tip of the blade wend its way through the small space where the double doors connected. She watched it slide down to jimmy open the lock.

She slid across the room through another door, one of a set of three, and closed it quietly as she entered another rehearsal room. Mirrors reflected her image at every angle. She scanned the room and noticed a large cabinet near the corner.

Nancy's movements felt amplified by the mirrors as she slinked around. She didn't have much time. One of the studio doors slammed. That meant the killer was in the room just outside. Another flash of lightning illuminated Nancy's room through the windows above, creating a maze of reflected light.

Nancy saw a small podium tucked against a far wall. She ran to the cabinet and opened one of its doors, ever so slightly, then dashed over to the podium and folded herself into the small space at the bottom.

As she was pulling in her leg, the door to the studio opened. Nancy stared into the reflection of the mirror angled at her. With the lights out, she could barely see herself, much less the room. Blood pulsed through her head. She stifled her own breathing with a hand over her mouth.

From another reflected angle, she watched her pursuer enter the room and stop. He carefully looked around, and she wondered who it was. Why he was doing all of this.

He eyed the podium, and she was suddenly sure that whoever was behind the mask had seen her. Nancy's eyes widened, and she hoped. Hoped he would leave. Hoped that, if he didn't, he'd do whatever terrible thing he had planned quickly and painlessly. She let tears flow.

Lightning flashed nearby, and the thunder followed immediately. It started with a small crackle, like popcorn kernels being poured into a hot pan, and culminated in a painfully loud boom.

Nancy could not tear her eyes from the man with the knife. In a flash, he sprang onto the cabinet, just as she had hoped. She would wait until he was next to the cabinet, and when he threw the door open, Nancy would unsqueeze from the podium, run for the door, and flee outside.

It was a good plan, a strong plan.

Nancy watched the killer exit the room. Then, she waited.

And waited.

She wasn't sure how long she sat silent, her arms cramped, her legs asleep and filled with tingling numbness. *Minutes*, she thought. *It has to be only minutes.*

She waited for one more streak of lightning before she dared move. When it came, and she saw no one, she slowly unfurled herself from the podium. She almost didn't care if a knife waited for her as the blood rushed back to her legs.

Nancy dragged herself up and pushed her back against the cool mirrored wall. She slid quietly along it, feeling as if every step toward the door left her two steps farther out of reach.

She didn't even dare sigh. She listened for footsteps, or doors opening, anything to signify that she should chance leaving the building.

There was a sound, then. It was not doors closing. It was not feet shuffling. The sound was so loud Nancy could feel the bass frequencies pass through her body in an undulating wave. It was the first time she had ever heard and felt music that did not make her want to dance. She screamed in terror, turned, and ran, no longer caring that she might be heard or seen. She ran right into the killer's grasp.

A gloved hand wrapped around Nancy's throat before she could suck in a full breath, and her body panicked for air. She flailed her tired arms and her tingling legs. The attacker's other hand sideswiped her face with the butt end of the knife, dazing her. She raised her head slowly and looked into the mask.

At my killer, she thought.

She really did wish, so close to the end, that she could learn who it was. She thought of reaching out to pull off the mask, but her eyes closed as she was overcome with a lightness, a feeling of floating. This feeling ended as her body was hurled through the air, and she slammed into the mirrored wall with such force that it shattered and rained down onto Nancy, who could do nothing to protect her face or body from the piercing shards.

She heard herself cry. She was back with the world, but not long for it. This she knew, as she looked up at the terror above her. She tried to scream, to tell the killer to stop. She wished for her own bed back home.

Then Nancy felt the pain of the knife puncturing her gut, and she whimpered as the blade twisted. It hurt, and it made her sad as she looked up at the killer, to imagine the smile behind the mask.

Nancy felt warmth leave her body. She felt everything turn bloody. She felt everything turn black.

Then she felt nothing.

Back in the archives, Max followed as Layna led him swiftly through corridor after corridor, her long legs pushing to the limit.

"I just don't think it's a good idea that he's alone," Layna said, not looking back.

It bothered Max that she was upset about Dillon. After all, they were trapped on an island and horrific things were happening to their friends. He had seen Alice. They all had seen Crosby. Max didn't know for a fact that Dillon was the killer, but Layna's failing to see that it *could* be Dillon irked him. He had to admit that it *could* be Daniel or Nancy or Parker or Mrs. D. or McKenna. Or a random person they didn't know. Everyone was a suspect. He wondered who thought it might be him. Did Layna?

"And I didn't think it was a good idea to leave you alone with him," Max responded. He reached out to grab her arm. She turned around, and a long, lightly curled lock of her brown hair fell in front of her face. He brushed it away with his hand, then bristled when she seemed to scoff at his touch. He hoped it was nerves. "Listen, listen, listen," he pleaded, softening his tone. "We're in this together. And if you wanna hate me because I'm doing what I think is best for you, for us, then go ahead. But I'm doing this because I love you."

Her steely regard softened.

"I just don't know what to think," she admitted, "or what to do. What's right or wrong."

"Welcome to the club. I don't really know what to do, either, I guess. But I know I wanna keep you with me. Keep you safe."

Max let her melt into his embrace. He kissed the top of her head, and though he couldn't tell, he hoped she smiled. His hands caressed her arms as he stepped back. "Now, what are we doing back here?"

Layna shook her head. "Crosby," she said, pausing to swallow his name, which clearly affected her. "He told me he would help by looking stuff up about my mother. If he found anything, it would be here."

They looked around at the aisles, file cabinets, and tables. Layna shrugged, but Max eyed something. He grabbed her hand and, this time, took the lead. "Wait a minute." They were at a table with boxes, papers, and a yearbook on it. "Bingo," Max said.

They shuffled things around, pulled items from the boxes, and skimmed through the yellowed pages of the yearbook. "Woah," Max said, pushing a newspaper in front of Layna. The front page stared back at them, filled with an image of people staring at the old theater building on fire as jets of water shot at the flames. The headline screamed out:

Tragedy Strikes Idyllic School

Layna gingerly picked up the paper, as if it might simply disappear were she not so careful. Her eyes darted back and forth, scanning the article.

"Listen to this," Layna said. "The prestigious and, some would say, mysterious Trask Academy of Performing Arts has endured what may be its most dramatic moment ever, a fire that sadly claimed the life of one of its young stars. The student, Amanda Kincaid, was said—" She stopped reading and dropped the paper. "Oh, my God." Her eyes filled with tears.

"Babe, I'm sorry. I— What do we do now?" Max wondered.

Layna tore off the front page of the newspaper. Grasping it tight, she turned and started moving faster than Max thought she could.

"Where're you going?" Max's voice dropped at the end, which turned the question into a slight accusation. He knew where she was headed, and why, and he was pretty sure she knew he knew.

The tattered front page of the newspaper slammed down onto McKenna's desk with a force that sounded like it could have shattered Layna's hand. She would not have cared if it had.

It didn't seem possible that Layna could feel more infuriated. Her friends had been targeted by a killer. The school had not done anything to protect them. She had uncovered the twisted secrets of its past that led, she had to assume, to the death of her mother. But there was a level beyond what she already felt, and it hit her when the dean barely glanced at the paper not just as if it were old news, but as if it weren't news at all.

"Ah, Ms. Curtis, I wondered when we might be seeing you," he gloated.

Layna took a deep breath and leaned in. "I'm not sure who you mean, Mr. McKenna. My name is Kincaid. Layna *Kincaid*." She spat the last name.

McKenna nonchalantly took off his glasses and wiped them with a blue pocket square.

"Now you're going to tell me what my mother had to do with all of this." Layna leaned back. Max stood at her side.

"Not just your mother, I'm afraid," McKenna said.

"Stop talking in riddles!" Max exploded.

Layna appreciated the defense but put her hand on his arm. She wanted answers, and yelling at the man who was at the root of the problem would get her nowhere.

McKenna stood and faced Max. "Raising your voice will not

get me to speak of things about which I do not know. If you want to understand what happened and, perhaps, why, I suggest, Layna," he turned to her coolly and leaned forward, "that you talk to your *mentor*."

Layna shook her head, confused. "Mrs. D.? Why would I talk to her? How could she—"

"You will find she is full of surprises," McKenna interrupted.

Layna turned to Max, running both of her hands through her hair. "Let's go."

"Layn, wait. What? Why?" Max asked.

"You heard him. And I'm betting Mrs. D. has more to say than our esteemed dean would ever want her to."

McKenna looked visibly shaken.

Layna was glad. "Yes, to be clear, sir, that was a threat. It's time to see what secrets you're holding on to."

Layna grabbed Max, and the two turned to leave. They made it only a few steps before McKenna spoke again.

"Mister Reynolds," the dean said, "it might be a good idea, while the ladies are speaking, that I borrow your technical expertise to fix the broken radio."

"Really?" Max wondered. "I'm starting to question your judgement, Harlan."

The dean blanched at the sound of his first name, but Max continued. "Staying here while Layna wanders off alone sounds like a bad idea."

"Why would it," the dean answered casually, "when you have been thinking for quite some time that I might be the one at the helm of all this—"

Layna waited for him to say it. Death. Murder.

"Misfortune," McKenna finished.

Layna closed her eyes, dismayed. "Max, I'll be fine. I promise." She saw worry in his eyes, a silent plea to get out of there together, to run away together, to hide together.

"You do want to get off the island, don't you?" McKenna asked.

"I'd settle for simply getting away from you, to be honest," Layna said. She hated the dean for so many things, but she knew he was right. She did need to get off the island.

But first she had to talk to D'Arcangelo.

CHAPTER XVI

Layna hurried across campus. She was being careful, she thought. She was also angry. With everything that had happened to her friends, she had failed to think of her family. She would have to confront her grandparents, of course. She knew that much. And it wasn't going to end well, she also knew that. They'd had a perfect relationship before. Now it was shattered. How could she ever trust them again, after such a heinous lie? Being misled her whole life was not something she could just brush off and forgive. Not this time. This wasn't her grandmother not letting her have more dessert. This wasn't her grandfather telling her she had better not climb the tree again. This was not an omission of the truth.

It was a scathing, scandalous, murderous lie.

As she mulled over what she would say, and how she would say it, Layna felt she was being watched. It raised the hairs on the back of her neck, and the muscles in her jaw tightened. She heard footsteps keeping pace, getting faster, getting closer.

She looked at the buildings in the distance. Could she make it?

But then Layna surprised even herself. She clutched her keys and turned to face her pursuer.

"Dillon!" she screamed. "What are you doing? You scared me." And he had. For the first time in a while, she was not happy to see him. She had hoped to make it across campus to D'Arcangelo's office without incident. It would have been better had she not run into anyone.

"Nice to see you, too," Dillon responded. "I can't find anyone."

Layna watched him, wondering if he didn't understand, or was just actively ignoring her.

"I went to look for Nancy after she left and you and Max ran off," Dillon continued. "She's not around, at least not where I can find her. And Daniel is missing, too. So is Max."

A pang of fear and maybe a tiny bit of guilt struck Layna when she heard Max's name. "What do you mean he's missing?" she asked. "He's with the dean right now, trying to fix the radio. I just left them." Dillon looked bewildered. "What are *you* doing?"

"Looking for you," Dillon said. "I lost you after you left the archives."

Any feeling of comfort because Layna was talking to Dillon instead of running from a killer left when she heard that. She stepped away from him. "How did you know I was even there?"

Dillon grabbed her arm. "Please, just listen to me, I followed you. I needed to make sure—"

"Don't touch me!" Layna yelled, pulling her arm away. Two red trails appeared where Dillon's nails raked her bare skin. And she ran, not looking back.

"Layna, stop! You don't understand! I can help you!" Dillon yelled after her to no avail. He watched her disappear into the darkness of the campus. He squinted and strained to keep his eyes on her. Then he saw something else, also off in the distance, closer to Layna.

Someone in dark clothing.

Moving in the same direction as Layna.

In a mask.

Layna stepped into the administrative offices breathless. She finally looked behind her and was relieved. Dillon was nowhere to be seen.

She pushed back strands of sweaty, sticky hair that clung to her forehead and the sides of her face, trying to compose herself before going in to D'Arcangelo's office. The light was on in there. Layna could see someone stirring through the translucent glass.

She put her hand on the cool, brushed metal door handle and pushed it down. Her stomach dropped as the door opened. *This is it*, she decided. D'Arcangelo would come clean.

Layna slinked inside, though her mind was screaming. She expected to see D'Arcangelo filing, or writing, or whatever it was teachers did when they weren't with their students. Instead the woman stood behind her desk, staring at Layna. Through her. Layna didn't care. What more could this woman do to make matters worse?

"I want to know why," Layna demanded as she stepped forward. "Why would you have kept any of this from me?"

D'Arcangelo moved from behind the desk, slid past Layna, and stopped at the door.

Layna watched and waited for the teacher to do something. To say something. The deadbolt clicked, a sound that seemed a thousand times louder than it should have been. A sound that sent a shudder through Layna. The door was locked. They were alone.

"I want to hear you say it," Layna demanded.

D'Arcangelo leaned against the door as she spoke. "It wasn't my choice," she muttered. "And before you think it, not even Dean McKenna's, really. We were—"

"You were what?" Angry veins pulsed in Layna's forehead. "What?"

"We were under strict orders from your grandparents to say nothing."

"You're lying."

"I wish I were," D'Arcangelo said. "The records were sealed

when you were a baby. This was their wish. We simply complied."

Layna felt as though she might fall. She stepped back and leaned on the edge of the desk behind her. "But I have a photo of my mother. I'm a little kid. I don't remember the picture being taken, but it's real. It's my mother."

"No, it's not. That I know," D'Arcangelo said. "Layna, listen, I don't think—"

"Nobody thought, that's the problem!" Layna regained her strength, and she could see that it shook D'Arcangelo, but she didn't care. "Secrets always come out, and the one person you hope to protect ends up being the one you hurt the most. And all because of the lies. Yours, the dean's, my grandparents', and whoever the hell else. Mrs. D., please, you have to tell me the truth. All of it. People are dying. My friends are *dying*. And I don't know how long I'll be safe."

D'Arcangelo sighed as she went toward the office's back windows. She looked out as she spoke. "Before I became a teacher here, I was a student," D'Arcangelo said. "A drama student, truth be told. I thought I'd make it. I really did. I left for a while, for years, and tried. Clearly, I failed. But this place, it has a power. It drew me back in. I worked at the school as a stage manager while getting my teaching credential. A cliché, believe me, I know."

Layna listened with genuine empathy.

"I was there," D'Arcangelo mumbled. "The night your mother was killed."

Layna sucked in her breath. But she needed to know more, to know everything. And in order to make it through, she had to be strong.

She watched as a tear dripped slowly down D'Arcangelo's face. "Your mother was all the things you were told. Beautiful, gracious, kind, and so, so talented. A shining star about to rise. And then, the tragedy. You were never told because your grandparents, the school, we wanted to protect you. I see now that what we've done is worse."

"Protect me from what?"

D'Arcangelo wiped away the tear and chuckled. "It sounds so wrong now, the truth," she admitted. "Your mother died in that fire, yes. And the old theater was a magnificent structure, so grand the school couldn't see it go even after it burned, so the alumni donated money to reconstruct it." She paused. "We found her, your mother, in the orchestra pit. She had burned to death."

Tears fell from Layna's eyes, but she did not wipe them away. She hoped they would cleanse the dread, though there could never be enough tears for that. She managed a steady voice. "Go on, please."

D'Arcangelo stepped back from the window and past Layna to the door.

Layna wondered if she was just going to leave. "You have to tell me. Whatever you know, everything you know. Whatever good you think is being done by hiding it, we're way past that!"

D'Arcangelo's hand eased up on the door handle and she turned around, a look of resignation on her face. "Oh, Layna, it's not that simple," she said. "What you don't understand is—"

The door's window shattered inward as a gloved hand burst through, fragments of glass shooting outward. Layna covered her face. D'Arcangelo tried to scream but was forcefully pulled back against the door frame. Layna saw her eyes. They looked sorry. Resigned. D'Arcangelo closed them as a polished blade appeared through her throat, then ripped upwards in a sick flash of metal, bone, flesh, and blood.

"No!" Layna squealed, her hands raised to her head as if it were about to fall off. She stood motionless, a grimaced look of pain and terror strapped to her face as blood sprayed onto her as the knife ripped out of D'Arcangelo's neck.

D'Arcangelo kept trying to say something in fits and spurts and gurgles of blood. She slid against the door and flopped lifelessly to the floor, like a marionette whose strings had been cut.

Layna wanted to scream as the killer reached for the door handle. Layna caught her breath when she noticed that the door was locked, and that the space in the window was too small for anyone to fit through. But her relief was short-lived as the killer yanked keys from D'Arcangelo's pocket.

Layna panicked. In moments, the killer would be inside. The twisted theatrical mask looked up, and the killer raised the keys and waved them at her, wiggling them back and forth as if in front of a child.

Layna looked for a way out as she heard the keys placed into the lock, one by one by one. When she heard a perfect connection, and the twisting of the doorknob, Layna knew she had one option.

Grabbing the heavy wooden chair from behind the desk, she raised it as far as she could and hurled it against the glass of the office windows. They shattered outward, as the chair fell back to the floor. She pushed it toward the killer, who was now in the office. He went down slicing the air toward Layna.

She did not stay to watch. As the killer struggled to get his legs unwrapped from the swiveling bottom of the chair, Layna climbed up on the inside ledge below the window. She yelped as her hands raked against the jagged shards still jutting from the casements. She ignored the pain and jumped, out and down, falling just a few feet and rolling when she hit the muddy ground. She looked up and saw the killer staring at her from the window, then got to her feet quickly.

She ran on the wet grass, her mind still on the bloody mess of Lillian D'Arcangelo. She looked back as she ran. No one in the window, no one behind her. No one after her.

She thought of going back to the security office and Daniel, or trying to find Nancy. Or Max or even the dean, or Parker. Somebody. It dawned on her that the last person she had thought of was Dillon. Why, she wasn't sure, but those feelings could be sorted out later.

She whipped her head back to look behind her.

And screamed.

It was Dillon. He grabbed Layna. She tried to pull away from him, but he held her too tight. "Layna, stop!" he yelled.

But she would not stop, not until she could get away. She tuned him out, his voice a clouded ringing in her ear. Then she yanked a hand free and slapped him across the face.

Dillon let her go, clutching at his cheek.

Layna looked at him as she backed up. He appeared hurt. Not physically, but deep down, somewhere else. As if she had done something he'd remember and hold against her. It was a look she had never seen on him before. And she didn't want to stay around to see what might come after it.

"Layna!" A voice, but not Dillon's.

She glanced behind and saw Parker. Flooded with relief, she ran to him.

Parker picked up speed. "What's going on? Where have you been?"

"Detective, stop!" Layna yelled. "It's him. It's Dillon. He killed Mrs. D'Arcangelo and now he's after me!"

Something flashed in Dillion's eyes. Something deeper than hurt. Anger, confusion.

"What? Layna, stop it," he said. "That's not true! I was trying to protect her!"

"He tried to kill me!" Layna yelled as Parker arrived.

The detective grabbed Dillon. "I've got him."

Dillon resisted, but Parker was much bigger, much stronger. Dillon jumped and heaved his body to the side, but Parker tightened his hold around Dillion's arms.

Layna squinted in sympathy.

"Settle down, young man," Parker demanded. "Come on. Both of you."

Layna let Parker lead. As he passed her, Dillon again gave her the look. It burned through her. She hated the way it made her feel. Like she was wrong. Or bad. Dirty.

She looked away and hoped Dillon didn't see the tears in her eyes.

Parker used Dillon as a makeshift battering ram to burst through the entryway of the security office. Layna entered behind them. She was upset, angry at Dillon. She suspected him, but deep down, she still didn't want to see him hurt.

Parker shoved her ex into a small room with a thick, wire mesh door. Seeing Dillon there made her feel like the island truly was a prison in so many ways. The door to the cage slammed shut with a loud clang. Parker locked it, throwing the keys on the desk.

"This is insane. I didn't do anything!" Dillon yelled.

Layna averted her eyes.

"That seems to be the mantra this weekend," Parker said. "I suppose if no one has done anything, we're in the clear, and two young girls are not dead!"

"Dammit!" Dillon screamed. He slammed a fist into the mesh.

Layna jumped. She was not at ease, even with Dillon behind a locked door.

Dillon took a deep breath and tried to explain. "I saw someone wearing a mask and I tried to follow him. But I lost him."

"Maybe you lost him because the person you were searching

for was you." Layna let the sarcasm slip through without regret.

"That's not true," Dillon said, shaking his head.

Layna stared at him, waiting to see if he would break. The tension was thick, palpable.

"Enough," Parker said. He looked at Dillon. "You're not going anywhere."

"He's safe in there, right? Secure, I mean?" she asked Parker. The detective nodded. "Then I'm going to find out once and for all what's going on."

"Not a good idea," Parker uttered, putting his head down.

"Then stop me."

Parker looked to Dillon, then back to Layna.

Neither of them could do much to stop her.

So she left to find her friends.

And the truth.

CHAPTER XVII

Layna stood outside the administrative building, near a stone time capsule from 1888. It was etched with a name that every student heard time and time again: Cadogan Trask. She wondered what secrets were hidden inside, and could they possibly be graver than what was happening. If she could, she'd have busted it open to see. After all, she had already defaced school property. What could they do at this point?

Layna hurled the rock in her hand and it smashed through the window of the records office. It was the second window she had broken; the first to get out, and now, to get in.

She stepped up to the building and pulled her sleeves over her hands as makeshift gloves. She hoisted herself up and shimmied her way through. It was never as easy as it was in the movies, she thought, where characters easily leapt up, slid in, and landed on their feet without making a sound.

Layna grunted as she tried to maneuver herself in a way that would not only be safe, but quiet. The leg of her jeans caught the edge of the window casing, yanking her back. She tumbled onto the floor. Her hands, still covered by sleeves, felt the crunch of glass, but it did not pierce through to skin.

"Dammit!" she yelped. The impact hurt. It would bruise.

But she was inside.

She rubbed her clothed hands together to rid them of any small shards, then brushed off her legs and butt. Reaching for the light switch, she found it did nothing. She tried again, but the power was out. It worked in the other buildings, and the storm had passed, so someone wanted to keep things in the dark. Literally, she thought.

She had things to do, and fast, so she started toward a set of file cabinets. She scanned the small placards on each, looking for the one with last names that started with G. She found it, and was ready to yank it open and rifle through its contents, but something stopped her. She caught herself still believing in the lie.

Her hand went down to the drawer marked K. Kincaid was her real last name. She was not a Curtis. The school knew it. And now so did she. She grasped the handle, her thumb pressed the little knob. She clicked and pulled and hoped it wasn't locked.

It wasn't. That took Layna by surprise, but she kept going, ravenous to learn more about herself. She flicked through manila folders, dingy with age, their stickers creased and peeling. She hoped to find a file on her mother, but there was nothing. And then she found her own. It was as if there were an electric charge when her fingers touched it, like the folder wanted to be in her hands. She ripped it out and slammed the drawer shut.

With one swift turn, she laid the folder on top of the cabinet. She flipped through page after page, seeing her grades, letters of recommendation, certificates, and awards. Everything she already knew about the girl she was. Or once was. She flipped another page and saw small tabs behind it. She went right to the one labeled, "Official Records" and pulled it out.

Dingy yellow greeted her, but there was nothing under the tab.

The papers had been ripped out.

Her birth records were gone. Her real identity was gone. *Not gone,* she thought. *Stolen.* She wasn't even real on paper.

But there was no time to mourn the loss, or wonder who could have taken the records. She heard a noise. Her body jolted with fear. She could feel the rush of acid in her stomach. Who would be in here besides her, unless they were there for her? She closed the file and decided to worry about the missing records later.

As she grabbed the folder at its edge, she accidentally bumped it. It took less than a second for her mind to understand what was happening before her body could react, and she watched the folder slide backward and fall behind the cabinet against the wall. The whoosh and thunk felt like a slap.

"Dammit!" she cursed, looking around as the noise came closer and closer. There was no time to pull the file cabinet from the wall, squeeze her arm behind it, grab the folder, and pull it back in one piece.

A shadow appeared in the hallway, just outside the door. Layna ducked, out of instinct, and frantically scanned for a way out, a place to hide, something.

She found it a few feet away, a side door that connected the Records Office to the next office, whatever it was. More administration, probably. She hoped the door was open and that the adjoining room had an exit. She scurried on her knees to the side door, reached for its handle, and turned. It gave, and she opened the door just enough to squeeze through. When she was on the other side, she heard the clicking of her escape door latching as the stranger opened the entrance door to the room she had just left.

Layna let out a muffled sigh. Thinking. Planning and plotting. She needed to do something, and fast.

With the lights out, she knew she could quietly move toward the other door. As she scuttled across the floor, she looked behind her but could neither see nor hear anyone, so she moved toward the next door until something on the floor caught her eye. It was a piece of torn paper, sitting near the edge of the desk. It looked blank, so she turned it over. Scrawled in handwriting she did not recognize, it said:

When the bough breaks the cradle will fall

The paper picked up the sweat from her hand as she rolled the words in her mind. Was it meant for her? Was it about her? She turned her head and saw that something reflected the tiny bit of moonlight that came through the casement windows. It was under the desk, so she ducked her head and peered below, but the space was too small to make anything out. She shifted herself past and around the far side of the desk when her hand landed on it.

A black shoe, shined to perfection. Her hand felt the softest wisp of fabric. A pant leg. Her eyes trailed upward to meet another pair of eyes, staring at her. She sucked in air, and as she let it out, a small, pained bleat came with it. She covered her mouth as tears fell from her eyes and collected at the tops of her fingers.

Her head shook back and forth, and she squinted, knowing she would not be able to hold back the scream that bubbled forth, waiting to cry out in madness because of the thing staring back at her.

The sawed-off head of Dean McKenna.

It sat perfectly in his own lap, and the dead man's hands cradled it like a small child. Sinews of flesh splayed out in a jagged mess that suggested, however impossible, that it may very well have been ripped off his body. The dean's dark pants glistened with blood which soaked through to his pale, old man skin.

She stared in shock. The dean, first a suspect, then a threat, was now a victim. Layna's scream erupted and rumbled through the tiny room, just as the door behind her opened, as if the sound of her terror were the catalyst.

The killer filled the doorframe.

Layna scrambled to get up, her blue Chuck Taylor's sliding in the slaughtered dean's blood. As her pursuer took a step closer, she found traction and bolted through the door connecting the offices. In the next room, she saw timecards scatter from a table to the floor as she flew through. Another door awaited, and she prayed it would open like the first.

It did. As she burst through it, she looked back and saw the attacker following. Not as fast as she might have thought, but rapidly enough.

Layna went from door to door and room to room. Four rooms later she had reached the end. There was nowhere to go but through the main door to the last office. Somehow, she knew it would be locked, and when she checked, it was. She grabbed a chair behind the only desk in the room, and a cardigan sweater that reeked of stale cigarettes fell off the back. The scent made her gag as she flung the chair at the glass. Broken lucky window number three. She let the chair drop back to the floor and grabbed the sweater, wrapped it around her arm, and used it to clear the jagged shards still stuck into the frame. Unraveling the material from her arm, she threw it to the floor, climbed through the window, and stretched her legs taut so she could land unhurt.

Once inside the hallway, Layna looked back into the room but saw nothing. She gazed back toward the hallway and barely missed the swinging knife. She pulled her head back, and the knife stuck in the wood frame.

Mere inches away, the killer yanked on the blade and worked it free. Layna forced her foot into his groin, and he went down with a grunt. The knife fell free from the doorframe and clanked next to the masked face of the attacker.

Layna wasted no time in using the advantage. She bolted for the end of the hall, pushed open the double doors, and left the building.

She panted as she ran to the adjacent dance hall. When she

looked back and saw no one, she pushed open the front doors, and entered the darkness. She tried the lights, but they were out. She sensed something was wrong when she felt herself slipping, ever so slightly. Allowing her eyes to adjust, she bent down and saw blood. A lot of it. She stood slowly, and turned to face another stare, this time from the slit throat and intact head of a very dead Daniel.

This time a crying gurgle of defeat came out instead of a scream. It was all she could do when she suddenly thought Alice must surely be dead. And then it hit her.

Nancy.

Layna found the strength to shake off the nightmare of Daniel and look for her friend, assuming she was even in the building. She rushed down the hall, tugging on whatever doors she could find. They were all locked, so she rounded the corner and saw that the entrance to the main studio was not only unlocked, but propped open.

She entered the room of mirrors, the only light coming from the reflected moon through a skylight, bouncing to and fro. One of its beams shone down on Nancy. Layna ran to the crumpled girl.

"Nancy? Thank God!"

But when Layna made it to her, it was too late. She looked down at the brutally slain girl, stabbed to death with shards of broken mirror.

"No!"

Layna's tears fell as she stroked her friend's hair, moving thick, bloody strands from Nancy's face. Her eyes were still open, but Layna dared not touch them. She wept until her hand snagged something underneath Nancy's head.

It was a crumpled, blood-soaked piece of paper. Layna pulled it close, unraveled it, and studied the words scrawled on it.

It will take more than seven years to counter

the broken mirror of my heart

Layna threw it down and got to her feet. She was exhausted, and her mind felt like it had been jumbled.

"What—what do you want?" she asked as if the killer had arrived for conversation.

She sobbed and wiped her face with her sleeve, careful not to smear blood on her face. She felt the fight leaving her body. Looking down at her friend, she backed away.

And stopped when she bumped into somebody right behind her.

Layna screamed, jumped back, and fell over Nancy's dead body. Her hands were inches away from jagged shards of mirror. She looked up, breathless.

It was Max. "Layn, come on, we have to go."

Layna wasn't sure what to do. Her eyes darted from Max, to Nancy, and then back to him. Max extended his hand to her. She reached out, but it felt as if she grabbed the hand of a stranger. So many questions ran through her head. So much terror, betrayal. She wasn't sure what to do. Or who to trust.

"Now!" Max yelped as he yanked Layna up.

She felt her shoulder pop when he pulled, and she got lightheaded. She turned back to Nancy and let out a scream, then grabbed onto Max, pushing her face into his muscled shoulder. It felt good when he held her tight.

"Oh, God, Max. What is happening?" she asked, the words muffled and buried in his jacket.

Max pushed her away gently. "Layna, we have to leave here, *right now.*" He didn't wait for a reply, leading her out of the room and down the hall. She did not, could not, turn back to look at Nancy again, even though it would be the last time she'd ever see her friend.

As they made it outside, Max cautiously looked both ways, as if the two were crossing a street of horrors.

"The dean is dead," Layna said.

"I know," Max said, too nonchalantly for Layna's liking. He pulled her, but she yanked her arm back, and he whipped around. "What are you doing? Come on!"

Layna stood firm. "Where? Go where? How did you know the dean was dead? And where to find me?" She saw he knew what she was insinuating.

Max softened, and his shoulders dropped. "I was at the security office with Parker and Dillon. Parker didn't have any answers, and Dillon wasn't talking, so I left to find you."

"When?" Layna asked.

"When *what*, Layn? Jesus."

"When did you leave there?" Layna was trying to hide her worry, but wasn't doing a good job. She shook her head. "And how did you know about the dean?"

"I saw the window to the records building was smashed, so I went in," Max admitted. "I found him. It looked like something else had gone down, so I followed the open doors to the window and, like you, came to the dance building." He edged closer, but Layna backed away.

"Layna, it's not me," Max said. "I'm not hurting anyone."

She looked at him. Her pupils dilated as she took in his face, wanting so desperately to believe him.

"I love you. It isn't *me*!" Max insisted.

His answer seemed fair enough to Layna. True enough. Then her eyes suddenly went wide. Behind Max, the familiar, horrible mask of the killer came into view as the man wearing it raced wildly their way.

Layna screamed loud enough for the entire island to hear. To shake the very trees bare. "Max, behind you!"

Layna knew she should have yelled for them to run, or just started running, because Max just turned around. Too late. The knife arced over him and came slashing down across the front of his body.

Max turned back to Layna, shock splayed across his face, a thin line of crimson growing under his torn shirt. It grew wide fast. Max glanced down at it, too.

"Run!" was all Max got out.

And they did. Just as the knife came slicing toward Max again, he grabbed her arm and they took off.

Layna ignored the burn in her legs, not sure if she could keep Max's pace. A look behind her confirmed the killer was giving chase.

She and Max ran across the quad and darted around the corner of the arts building. The jingle of a student-crafted wind chime, forged from steel and bigger than the two lovers combined, greeted them.

Layna bumped into Max when he stopped. "What are you doing? Keep going!" she hissed.

Max spoke fast, so fast that Layna seemed to catch only every other word. She tried to focus on what he was saying as she watched him bleed heavily, the blood pooling at his skinny waist and trickling to the ground. To his sneakers. It crushed her, and she clutched at her chest as if she felt his pain.

"Leave me, just go," Max pleaded.

"What? No, Max—"

"Just do it," Max ordered. "He can't get us both if we're not together. Please, Layn." He bent over in pain.

Layna softly touched the top of his head, not even trying to hold back tears. "Jesus, Max, I'm so sorry. This is all my fault."

"Just go!" he said, and pushed her.

Layna knew, hoped, it was because he loved her. That's what

she told herself. Right then she remembered the film *Love Story*. It had been one of Nancy's favorites for its melodrama. She always went around saying love meant never having to say you're sorry, but now all Layna could think was love meant never having to get your boyfriend killed. But she backed away from Max slowly. "I love—"

The killer appeared around the corner. Layna watched as the knife hovered over Max again, about to lower. This time she did not let tears flow. Instead she used the anger collected deep inside her. "Hey, Asshole!" she yelled.

The attacker stopped and raised his twisted mask to her. She stared into the deep blackness where eyes should be.

"It's me you want. And this." She waved the manuscript tauntingly. It was a risk, but it was the only card she could play. She turned and ran. She did not see the killer hesitate, or Max's broad shoulders heave as he slammed a fist into the attacker's stomach, causing him to drop the knife and stumble back. Max moved awkwardly as well, losing more and more blood, but he managed to grab the knife.

When Layna thought she was far enough away, she looked back. Ready to tease with the manuscript, to scream at the killer to come take it.

But Max and the killer were gone.

CHAPTER XVIII

The corrugated metal door to the technical warehouse slid open. Weak and out of breath, Max pushed himself inside. Clutching his bloody chest with one hand, he used the other to pull the sliding door closed behind him. He leaned back against the cool metal and surveyed his wounds.

Around him were half painted sets, flats, scrims, equipment, machines, and wires. The building was not meant for public view, and everything was strewn about wherever it would fit. Max practically lived here, where he enjoyed building things, crafting vistas for the stage shows, using his hands.

Max crept farther inside. Dimly moonlit through the skylights above, he made his way through the tall shelves, stacks of tools, and ladders. His thoughts were lost in what to do next, and he did not notice the small drops of his blood that hit the concrete floor every few feet.

Crimson breadcrumbs.

As he made his way to a darkened corner, he heard the door slide open with a powerful screech. He ducked behind a series of painted landscapes and watched the silhouette of the killer fill the wide opening. Not wasting time, Max stretched his free arm above his head, trying to ignore the pain of extending his wound. He grabbed a set of bars connected to scaffolding above him, which led to a series of catwalks. If he could get up there, he could slink his way back toward the front of the building. Or, if not, maybe stay quiet and hide.

Then he felt his skin tear. He looked down with a wince and saw his blood on the floor. His gut flipped when he saw the trail of drops, and again when he saw the killer notice them.

The killer wasted no time. He followed the red trail to where Max hid, sprinting, his blade twisting until it came down, fast.

But it sliced only air.

Max was gone. Or, at least out of sight.

He watched the attacker look down and follow the blood drops in another direction. Max's impromptu decoy had worked, but he didn't think it would work for long. He was barely five feet overhead, clinging with his arms and legs to the scaffolding. Sweat beaded on his forehead. He knew he wouldn't be able to hold on for much longer. One of his legs started to slip, and he willed it to stay put even as his muscles screamed in protest.

He realized the leg was the least of his worries when he saw a single drop of blood hit the back of the killer's dark jacket. It soaked into the fabric without giving him away. But Max's relief was short lived. The killer took a first step and then *plop plop*, two red globules sailed to the floor in front of his path.

The mask tilted upward. Max let go and used his limp body as a weight to crush his pursuer. They both went to the ground and the killer's knife slid across the floor. Max watched it slide away and let out a yelp. The fall hurt more than he thought it would, but it worked. He scrambled off the killer, who was sprawled on the ground, kicked him in the head, and ran. The killer got to his knees, shook off the blows, grabbed the knife, and rose to his feet.

Max did not get far. He ducked under some equipment and tried to put a barrier between himself and the killer, but he was trapped. He looked back at the killer, who was shaking his head and pointing with the knife above Max.

Max had hid under a ladder. "Screw your bad luck!" he yelled in a rage. Adrenaline coursed through him and replaced the fear. "You want me? Come and get me!"

The killer obliged, sprinting toward Max, the knife pumping back and forth in his hand.

Max leapt as high as he could, higher than he ever had before. He grabbed the scaffolding with one arm, and his muscles burned, but they worked. Like a monkey, he threw his other arm above the first, and as he climbed, he then had his legs to boost himself past every bar he reached. He looked above him and knew, no matter how hard he tried, that he was too far from the next bar. He feared there was nowhere else to go until he saw a set of thick, bound wires connected to a light board high above. It was all he could do to grab it.

And then the scaffolding teetered violently. Max stared down and saw the attacker ramming into it, again and again. The entire mechanism swayed back and forth like a domino, deciding if it was going to fall or stay put.

Max knew what would happen.

With one more Herculean shove, the attacker got the scaffolding to give way. It hit the ground with a thunderous echo as Max dangled from the wires, using every bit of his waning strength to hang on. He grimaced as he tried to shake sweat from his eyes and matted hair from his forehead.

When he looked down, the killer was gone.

"He—Help! Somebody help me!" Max screamed.

He heard a clinking of metal on metal. The sound caused Max's heart to drop.

Above him stood the killer.

Max looked down. It was at least a twenty-foot drop. He could let go, but hitting the solid concrete floor would probably break both his legs, or worse. Instead, he tried to swing on the wires to maneuver himself to a lower point as the cables sagged under his weight. He inched closer to potential freedom as he swayed back and forth.

On the third try, it happened. The wires started to uncoil. Two of them snapped. Fear filled Max's eyes as he looked up at the watching killer, whose next move Max anticipated a moment before it happened.

"No. No, no, no!" he yelled.

It was no use. The killer reached for an electrical box, yanked it open, and flipped the switches.

With each circuit Max grew more afraid. And with each second, another wire seemed to snap, or threaten to.

Then the killer struck electric gold, and the stripped and broken wires in Max's grasp crackled and sizzled to life.

"Stop!" Max screamed.

The killer slowly shook his head. With gloved hands, he pulled the wires closer to him, which pulled Max closer as well. Max could go nowhere and do nothing as the killer yanked on his torn, bloody shirt, pulling him nearer still.

The knife came out, and Max knew it was over. He slid his hands along the wires until they reached a bare one. He screamed. The pulsing electricity lit up his nerves like acid coursing through him. Max started to shake, and he only let go when the killer stabbed him in the hand, the knife almost going right through the palm.

As he fell to the ground, Max watched the killer get smaller. The thick wires snapped altogether and flew back like a jungle vine. Sparks shot out, and small arcs of blue electricity shimmered in the dark.

Just before Max hit the ground, he thought of Layna, and he hoped she was still alive.

The doors to the security office burst open. One of them hit the wall as Layna rushed in, out of breath. She turned, shut the doors, and flipped the deadbolt. She put her hands on the door and leaned forward to rest.

"Hello?" a voice from behind asked, startling her.

Layna was shocked to see Dillon in the cage. "Dillon, Jesus, what are you still doing here? Where's Parker?"

"You should know. I'm a killer, right?" Dillon asked calmly.

Layna looked sheepishly at him. Dillon was locked up because of her. She shuffled toward him tentatively. "Dillon, look, I'm—"

"Sorry, yeah. Me too." He stared at Layna. "I didn't mean to scare you. Really."

"The killer is out there," Layna said, in a voice so quiet even she thought it sounded like a little girl's.

"Are you all right?" Dillon asked. "I don't know what's happening. Everyone else is gone. And I'm scared."

Layna let her guard down. It was the first time all evening she had a moment to think, to let her feelings wash over her. She took a deep breath, felt her throat tighten, and the room, and Dillon, blurred with tears. She did not blink. She did not want them to fall. Not in front of Dillon. Not when so much of this, she now knew, was her fault.

"I'm scared, too," Layna said. "Nancy's dead. And Max. I lost Max. We were together, but then the killer came after us, and Max got hurt. I don't know where he is. I don't even know if he's alive!"

Layna put her hands on the cage. She felt Dillon's warm touch through the metal grate. It felt nice. It felt safe. But she pulled away.

"Max is fine," Dillon said.

"How do you know?"

Dillon chuckled. "Because he's Max."

Layna remained stoic, even as Dillon let a small smile slip. But she could not stop her eyes from blinking. Tears ran down her cheeks in small rivulets. "Mrs. D. and the dean. They're dead."

Dillon looked surprised. "What?"

"They're all *dead*," Layna spoke through sobs. "What are we gonna do?"

Dillon clasped his fingers in the wire, pleading. "Layn, you have to help me get out of here. Please don't keep me trapped in here."

Layna stared at him. She just wasn't sure what to do.

"Where's Detective Parker?" asked Dillon.

"I don't know. I went to see Mrs. D. and McKenna about my mother. All the things I never knew. There was so much, Dillon!"

"Listen to me, when Crosby went off to do some looking, so did I," admitted Dillon. "I think that's why the killer grabbed me and used me to get to Crosby. He was going to kill both of us for what we found, but he didn't get a chance."

Layna sniffled and wiped her face of tears. She ignored the fact Dillon snooped into her records. She needed to know. "Crosby knew about the fire. What did you find out?"

Dillon rolled his head back in revelation. "There's so much more. Starting her junior year, your mother had a promising playwriting career, but she got pregnant."

This was new information to Layna, simultaneously shocking and not shocking. "With me," she said to herself.

Dillon went on. "She was dating some all-star guy from a school on the mainland."

"So?"

"So, *he* didn't get her pregnant," Dillon emphasized. "Some young teacher's aide from her writing class here did. Both of them knew that if the affair ever got out, all hell would break loose, so she left school, and then came back for senior year."

"How did she leave for a year? Wait." Layna began to put the pieces together. "Someone knew. Someone here knew. Mrs. D. tried to tell me, before she—she couldn't."

Dillon eyed her bag. "Your mom's play? She wrote it while she was away. She used her affair as an insurance policy so they'd give her the showcase. She also made them promise not to fire the aide. She loved him. And he loved her. She knew the school wouldn't want any scandal, so as much as McKenna hated it, he gave her the spot. And there was no way they could say no to her material. But when they read it, you better believe they were concerned."

"What happened to my mother?" Layna asked, though she feared she already knew.

Dillon's eyes softened. "She was rehearsing when the theater was set on fire. Layn, your mother was murdered."

Layna's eyes slammed shut, but there were no tears this time. Anger filled her. "All those years of hearing the story. All those kids hearing it before me. And we made fun of it. Like it was a game. Or a joke."

"Nobody knew, Layna, which was what the school wanted," Dillon said. "But something changed."

Layna pulled the play from her bag and paged through it.

"What you have there is all that was recovered from the fire," Dillon continued. "She wanted to use her talent to get back at the people who shunned her. Who made her feel worthless. She knew she made a mistake and wanted to make them pay like they made her pay."

Layna thought on all of this. So many lies, so much betrayal, and she was at the core. She stopped flipping pages as another thought crossed her mind. Something more telling. Something more worrisome.

"None of this was in the newspaper," Layna said, not looking up. She was afraid to watch him answer.

"I'm not going to pretend you don't already know what went on. I'm pretty sure you found your records."

Layna stared at him. This was going as she had thought it would, but not how she hoped it would.

"Of course you did," Dillon said. "I know you, Layn. Things were missing, right?"

Layna stepped outside herself and felt that if this were a movie, now would be the Hitchcockian shot where she seemed to float through the room as the background pulled away from her, as though the air were not only pulled from the room but yanked from her lungs. She felt suffocated.

"I told you, I'm here to help," Dillon said sympathetically. "Once you found the play and learned you were a part of this, I wanted to protect you. Whoever was after you would want to know how everything was connected." He paused and swallowed. "So I took the files. But only so no one else could!"

Layna held the play with one hand and let the other caress her arm, where she felt her skin crawling. What Dillon did was a violation, no matter the reason. "Then, it's true," she said.

"What?"

"Somebody out there is finishing what my mother couldn't. Teaching a lesson using the ideas she wrote. Making them happen."

She inched closer to Dillon, the look on her face one he hadn't seen before, a look she had never used before. Never had a reason to. Complete resolve wrapped in anger, wrapped in sorrow, wrapped in hatred.

"What are you doing?" Dillon asked.

Layna could hear the apprehension in his voice. "I'm gonna

find the keys. I'm letting you go. And then we're getting outta here."

Layna and Dillon stood at the locked front gates of the campus. They stared up at them, and Layna wished she could open them by sheer force of will.

"I can climb it," Dillon offered.

Layna shook her head. The idea, noble. The execution, impossible. "It's too high. And your arm." She did not know the exact medical status of his injured arm, but it was incapacitated. Dillon had walked along the fence, and when his arm brushed against a light post, it had made Layna wince as well, another reminder his pain was her fault.

"I can at least try," Dillon retorted.

And he did. He leapt up, then yelped in pain. There was just no way.

"Dammit," Layna said. "I'm not mad at you, I'm—"

"Mad at the dirt?" Dillon answered.

Layna smiled. Then she laughed. She thought back on the fleeting memories of how much fun she and Dillon had when they watched *Mommie Dearest*. She forced a heavy sigh.

As they walked Layna focused on the ground, stopping when she noticed two things that did not sit well with her. Dillon peered over her shoulder, then stood at her side so he, too, could see.

"Are those—?"

"Yes," Layna answered. Detective Parker's walkie-talkie. And his gun. She reached down.

"Jesus, Layn, don't touch it!"

Too late. Layna crouched to her knees and pulled the weapon from the grass. It was wet. From the earlier rains, she thought. Until she recognized it wasn't rain at all.

"That's blood!" Dillon said.

Layna answered with a stunned nodding of her head. She sat, momentarily mesmerized by the notion that she was trapped, at her own school, with a bloody weapon in her hand. She looked up at Dillon, but said nothing. What could she say?

A voice crackled to life through the walkie-talkie.

"Having fun, Miss Curtis? Oh, I'm sorry. Miss *Kincaid*," the voice taunted.

Dillon grabbed Layna with his good arm and hoisted her up, grunting in discomfort at the strain.

"Let's just go. Now," Dillon pleaded.

But Layna was fixated on the radio. The voice. It was him.

Again, the radio hissed. "Didn't your mother teach you any manners? I asked if you were having fun. I know *we* are."

The next voice that came forth triggered a mixture of fear, anger, hope, and helplessness deep within Layna. She knew the voice. Had felt it wash away her tears and fears during late nights.

It was Max.

"Screw. You!" Layna heard Max gurgle at his captor. Layna grabbed the walkie. It also had blood on it, but she did not care. All that mattered was Max was alive. Somewhere.

She frantically pushed the buttons.

"Max! Max? I'm coming!" she yelled. "Leave him alone, you son of a—"

"Now, now, we can't have such vulgar language from such a pristine girl," the voice of the killer interrupted.

"Listen to me—"

"It's you who'll do the listening!" The voice turned dark,

grating. Like coal dust and mud mixed with water, some terrible sludge. "It's time to finish things where they started. Get ready, Layna, the real show is about to begin. Your *mother* would be so proud."

Layna threw the walkie talkie into the brick wall in front of her. She hadn't thought of doing it. It just happened. Pieces of bloody plastic fell to the ground next to the silent device.

"Great," Dillon muttered. "Now what do we do? Where do we go?"

"My mother," Layna whispered. "My mother would be so proud." She looked over Dillon's shoulder. He turned around, and they both stared at what Layna knew to be their final destination.

The old theater building. It lingered like a shadowy backdrop of ashen paper. Without saying a word, Layna started walking. Dillon stood perfectly still. "Are you coming?" she said without turning back, the downturn in her voice at the end less a question and more a command.

"What are you doing?" Dillon asked, his own voice pitched higher than she had ever heard. He sounded afraid.

"I'm playing my part," she said. She opened the play in her hands and turned to face Dillon.

He gave no response, so Layna started walking again. She had finally comprehended her destiny in all of this. Whatever fate had in store, it had seemingly always had its eye on her. She felt like the fabled Cassandra, though she was not given the gift of prophecy. Layna could only hope the outcome would favor her. And Dillon. And Max.

She was roused from her thoughts when she heard Dillon jog to catch up.

Together they walked toward the theater.

Where the story began.

Where the legend grew.

Where the death continued.

And to where it would, for better or worse, end.

Layna looked tired, but not defeated. She held up the last page, half-full of writing, half blank, the yellowed, charred paper asking to be filled. “I’m going to finish what my mother started.”

CHAPTER XIX

Layna and Dillon were consumed by the shadow of the theater ruins before them. Plastic blew in the wind, occasionally caught on jagged pieces of lumber. Sawdust, mixed with soot from the fire ages ago, somehow still bled from cracks between the original boards, dancing in the wind. Layna eyed a small eddy.

As it whisked across the ground and blew itself out, Dillon asked, "Are you sure about this?"

"What choice do I have?" Layna retorted. She scrutinized the dark structure before her. It seemed to grow as she stared at it, defied it. It was now or never. It was time for her final act. To see this through, once and for all. For her mother and herself.

She turned back to Dillon with a cold stare. "Besides, what have we got to lose at this point?" She shrugged and headed into the darkness of the theater entrance. Just before she disappeared in the shadows, she turned to see a slack-jawed Dillon.

"What have you got to lose? Are you serious?" he asked.

Layna entered the empty remains of the building. It was like stepping into a flesh-stripped skeleton.

Dillon caught up to her. Layna felt him reach his hand down, and almost by instinct, she grasped it and interlocked her fingers with his. Even though pangs of guilt rushed through her because she was somehow offending the memory of her relationship with Max, Dillon's hand felt safe, familiar, and warm.

The two made their way through the maze of building

materials, saw horses, lumber piles, plastic sheets, and everything else the school's coffers had regurgitated to make this once shining beacon sparkle again. For Layna, though, no matter how beautiful the new structure would be, no matter how grand a show it could stage, the building would never be good. Never be right. It was a murderer that swallowed her mother whole in a terrible, painful grip of fire, solitude, and torment.

Dillon squeezed her hand and motioned toward the stage. The ghost light sat left of center stage, its white bulb burning brightly. A silent beacon for those alive or dead.

The wind howled, and they heard slight drops of rain falling on what was left of the roof. Where there was no covering, the droplets hit the concrete flooring, barren seats, and construction debris. The sound mixed with the crinkling of plastic tarps that caught the wind as it eked its way through the structure.

Layna thought she saw the killer's black outfit darting in and out between the black plastic sheeting that danced in the breeze. She stiffened and elbowed Dillon. He saw it, too. The mask dodged in and out of sight among with fluttering plastic.

Layna held the gun up.

"Woah! Woah!" Dillon exclaimed.

Layna was unfazed. She started forward, held the gun in front of her, and gripped it tight with both hands. "Follow me," she ordered.

"Layn, maybe you should—"

"Keep your voice down," Layna whispered. "We both know we're not alone."

She held the gun defensively with shaking hands as she and Dillon made their way down the aisle, where a few rows of new seats had been installed. There was also a refurbished orchestra pit and a brand new catwalk system high above, a virgin set of steel crossbars and girders that waited to be hung with lights and technical apparatus.

Layna squinted when she saw silhouettes in more than a few of the new seats. Silhouettes that shouldn't be there. When she rounded the first row, Layna let one arm drop to her side. The other, holding the gun, trembled.

Dillon dragged a few steps behind. "Layna, wait."

Layna gestured for him to stop talking. She understood what she saw. What might have been something out of a nightmare. In the seats, facing the stage, was an audience.

Layna's dead friends.

One by one, in the order in which they had been snuffed out, they sat, eyes wide, in what Layna knew to be final looks of terror.

Sydney. Alice. Crosby. Nancy. Daniel. D'Arcangelo. Dean McKenna.

Some were covered in blood. All were very much deceased. Layna ran toward the bodies out of need, out of desire, out of a primal urge to hold them one more time, to shake them, to make them come alive.

Dillon caught up to her and grabbed her. "Layna, no."

She struggled, though there were no more tears. Dillon stroked her hair and held her. She squinted away the image as best she could, tried to force it from her mind to forget having seen more dead bodies in an instant than anyone should have to see in a lifetime. In ten lifetimes.

Then she realized that Max was not there. Neither was Detective Parker. She pulled free of Dillon, wiped her nose with her forearm, and turned around. "Come out here and show yourself, you bastard!" she yelled.

There was no answer. Layna looked around, past Dillon. No one. Nothing.

And then an answer came, when the killer popped up behind her, raised the knife, and brought it down, slashing Layna's shoulder.

The wound drew blood. Layna dropped the gun and covered the slash with her hand. She watched as the weapon slid into the orchestra pit, then she ran.

But the killer gave chase, slashing with the knife fast enough that Layna could hear it. Too close. She ran in back-and-forth diagonals, hoping for an advantage. She stopped only when she saw tall sheets of raw plywood stacked against a wall. She ducked behind them, and the knife shredded the edges of the top layers, barely missing her.

It was dark in her makeshift hiding place, and frighteningly quiet. Layna pressed her back against the wall and shimmied through the tight space toward the middle. If the killer entered from one end she had a chance to escape in the other direction. Then, the knife short-circuited her thinking as it pierced the wood inches from her face. She screamed in surprise and terror.

The blade pulled back, and Layna edged toward it, predicting that the next time it would rush through where her head had just been. And it did, grazing her already stabbed shoulder.

"Ow!" she screamed, unable to help it.

Blood seeped from her shoulder. The knife partially retracted, the serrated edge stuck in the pulpy wood. Layna watched as it twisted back and forth. With each tug Layna saw the panels pull away from the wall ever so slightly. With her back pressed against the wall and hands pressed against the wood, she pushed with all her power.

The panels came free and toppled over onto the killer.

As the bottom edges of the panels rose, Layna leapt on top of them and literally ran over the killer underneath. She saw the knife slide to the floor, and barely thinking, she grabbed it, and ran.

"Dillon! Get out!" she yelled. She looked back and saw the wood shifting as whoever was under it tried to get out from its weight.

Layna turned back and kept running, making her way to the wings of the stage that were closest to her. She slid into the darkness and slowed down, trying to control her breathing, shallow from fear and exertion.

The killer was no longer trapped underneath the wood. She backed away silently. She used her hands to feel her way behind her and looked for, hoped for, the familiar shape of an exit door.

Instead, she felt someone standing behind her. She screamed and turned.

"Shhh!" Dillon said. He grabbed hold of her tightly.

"Dillon, listen—"

"Shhh," he repeated.

So not like Dillon at all, Layna thought. And then her eyes went wide. She understood, too late, that the grip of the boy she had almost once loved, and who she thought had loved her, was not one of protection. It was to restrain her. She fought the acrid taste of fear as it rose in the back of her throat.

"Dillon, stop, you're hurting me," she said quietly and, she hoped, calmly.

Dillon paid her plea no mind. Layna felt his fingers leaving red marks on her flesh, through her clothes.

He pushed her slowly backward. Where was he taking her? Where was he *forcing* her?

The dark gave way to more light as she was prodded on stage. The ghost light was blocked by a figure. The killer, a silhouette framed in an almost angelic light.

Layna pleaded with Dillon. "Please, don't do this. Dillon, stop!"

He dug his hands into her forearms harder. He clenched his teeth and shook his head. She didn't want to comply but was afraid to anger him more. She knew what an angry Dillon could be like.

Then Dillon let one of his hands go slack and took something from a holster under his shirt. It was the gleaming blade Layna knew must have torn into more than one of her friends, but there was little time to contemplate the idea or think about them. Dillon shoved her, hard. She flailed backwards and started to fall, but she stopped mid-air. The killer had caught her, like a horrifying version of the trust-fall challenge.

Layna pulled herself free and turned around. She crossed her arms to massage the spots where Dillon had held too tight, keeping her eyes trained on the deep, dark sockets of the killer's mask.

Who was under there?

Why?

The killer stepped forward, and Layna instinctively stepped back, but she was stopped when she bumped into Dillon. Both he and the killer were bigger, stronger, like a cage of flesh.

The killer's black-gloved hand rose and stroked the side of Layna's face. She hated the touch. It made the hairs on the back of her neck stand and chills run down her arms. Still, she worked hard to hide her fear and give her attacker no outward satisfaction. She stared at the eyes of her captor, squinting to make out who it was.

The hand at the side of her face grabbed her chin. Layna yelped in surprise at the force as it brought her face to theirs. Closer, closer, closer.

Layna's hand was forced by the killer to caress the mask and her fingers reluctantly traced over the intricate grooves and curves. It was some sort of plastic, or metal. Smooth and shiny. She felt warmth as her fingers got closer to its mouth and hot, moist breath wisped around her hand.

"Go ahead, Layna," Dillon said, with a saccharine glee. "It's what you've been waiting for. The big reveal."

Layna silently agreed. She did want to know. Slowly, her hand slipped to the underside of the mask. She slid her fingers under its front edge and pulled upward.

The mask glimmered in the light as it fell to the stage floor. Layna followed it with her eyes, seeing it land and rock slowly before coming to a stop. The empty eye holes still stared blankly at her. She lifted her head and adjusted her gaze.

And when Layna, the girl who had been at the root of so much pain, so much blood, looked into the killer's eyes, her own were not filled with surprise or shock, or even fear.

They were filled with absolute fury.

"Detective Parker?" she questioned venomously. "I trusted you. Why did you do this to us? To me?" She tried to lunge toward Parker, but Dillon yanked back on her shoulders from behind.

Rage filled Layna's eyes. She didn't have a specific plan, just anger.

Parker fingered the blade in his hand. "Poor, innocent, put-upon Layna. You never were able to see the big picture," he taunted. "Do you *still* not get it?"

Hovering behind Layna, Dillon inched his mouth closer to her ear. She felt him suck in breath. "I don't think she gets it."

Parker turned around and took a few steps, contemplating. "I know, the detective as bad guy. How *boring*." He turned back to Layna. "But you always want to have a twist or, as your poor friend Crosby might say, something up your sleeve. And that's where it gets a little more interesting. You see, I'm not a cop, or a detective. I'm just a guy who knew this perfect school and its perfect existence would never, ever want any bad press, so I forged a few documents, made a few phone calls, and hopped on the ferry to help investigate the latest in a long line of problems here at McKenna's little enclave. He wouldn't have checked anything out himself. In fact, he wanted me gone before I even got here. The tricky part was making sure he didn't recognize me."

Layna cocked her head. She wondered whether, if she looked

hard enough, she might recognize him. But she didn't. She couldn't.

"Thank God the old bat didn't scrutinize me as much as you're doing right now," Parker said. "I knew I had him licked when he didn't give me a second glance. And it was so easy! All it took was different hair color, a different cut, and a lot of time at the gym. You see, everyone bought that I was a cop, one of the good guys. And I used to be a good guy. I was a teacher. A writing instructor. Okay, fine, fine, fine, a teacher's aide, to be exact. Right here at this very fine, very exclusive, very special place."

Layna didn't like where this was going.

"And I knew your mother," Parker admitted playfully.

Layna stared at him, her mouth slack. Too many thoughts and possibilities and scenarios swirled in her head.

"Oh, it's true," Parker continued. "I did. Your mother and I knew each other. *Intimately*."

Layna struggled against Dillon's hold, but he was too strong. "You're lying," she spat at Parker.

"Why would I do that? Sweetheart …" he said in a voice that sickened Layna. He brought his face so close to hers, she felt his hot, rank breath. "My blood," he said in a measured, terrible way, "flows through your veins."

The very idea was too much for Layna. Her head wobbled back, her eyes closed. When she spoke, it was just one gurgled word that formed a bubble of spittle and then broke as she uttered, "No."

Parker looked at Dillon, who still held on to Layna and smiled back conspiratorially.

"No matter how many times you say no, it won't stop it from being true," Parker continued. He circled Dillon and Layna. "After the scandal of Amanda's—excuse me—your *mom's* pregnancy, I got fired. But that's not what ticked me off. You see, what really got me was the prank. A little, deadly prank."

Parker once again faced Layna. She stared back at him through red-veined eyes. How much more awfulness could there be in this night? In her past?

"I think she has questions," Dillon said.

"And I have answers," Parker said flatly. "Your mother was on stage trying to perfect her monologue. A monologue she wrote."

Layna listened carefully, simultaneously hating and loving the words, the last moments of her mother's life, narrated by a monster.

"She must have been focusing on the pages in her hand," Parker continued, "not seeing the eight alumni, just a year out of school, shuffling around backstage. They thought it would be funny to light smoke bombs in the theater. Scare the slutty girl who banged a teacher, left to have a baby, and came back to take the top spot from their friends."

Parker snaked closer. Layna felt a wrath surging within him. She imagined dark, pungent wisps of fury seeping out from his pores. She closed her eyes, partly to shut away the visual, but also to recapture the image of her mother .

"They were all drunk," he resumed, "sucking on a bottle of whatever they could get their hands on. They tried not to laugh as they put smoke bombs on the floor. It must have felt strategic, but it was actually stupid. They set some too close to a pile of painters' rags from the night before. One by one they lit them, as your mother called out from the stage, asking who was turning the lights out. Bothering her. Toying with her. Tormenting her. But soon, it was the kids in the shadows who were terrified. Your mother probably had no idea what was going on until the smoke reached the front of the stage.

"The rags went up first in a blaze of heat. Then the scene flats buckled and burned. The flames zipped up the thin material, reaching the top and engulfing the curtains above. Your mother was imprisoned on stage as the world grew unbearably hot around her."

Layna cried with dry eyes as she imagined her mother trapped in the theater like she and so many friends had joked about for so long. It was no longer funny. It was no longer a myth, a legend, a story to be told on a dark and stormy night. It was real. It was her mother's life.

It was now her life.

And just then she was no longer cross with Parker, or Dillon, for her ire had been replaced with an insatiable need to find out who had killed this woman, her mother, who had given up so much.

Dillon's arm twitched on her shoulder, and Parker moved in closer still, forcing Layna back to the present.

"The kids left her on the stage as they ran out, slamming the exit door behind them," Parker continued. "It was too late for your mother. The fire had reached so far, and gotten so hot, that beams from above crackled. Heavy ropes burnt and snapped, and then the light rigs came crashing to the ground, blocking the exit. Your mother was going to die inside the theater. Inside the one place she had hoped to spend her entire life. Applause would turn to ash, and she would burn to dust."

Layna did not want to believe any of it, yet she knew it had to be true. Her mother's life ended in searing pain. The theater no longer held the story of a stranger, or a ghost, or a figment of overactive imaginations. It held the sordid tale of her mother's murder.

Parker described a small crowd gathered outside the theater, watching smoke pour from the building. People skittered back when windows shattered, and some screamed when the doors cracked and were pulled in by the raging, oxygen-sucking inferno.

Layna felt as though the fire were an evil, incarnate thing, a beast set upon taking her mother.

Parker spoke of a crowd watching the building glow red against the dark night. Watching the smoke billow up. Scrutinizing the glowing embers as they floated upward and transformed from a raging red to a cool gray in the misty evening.

And of how he was there, watching with all of them, but feeling something none of them could, because none of them had loved the girl trapped inside.

"I watched as the group of alumni pranksters ran as fast as they could from the back of the theater. No one else saw them as they blended into the fog. They had the gall to stand at the back of the crowd and stare in awe as the theater burnt down.

"No one tried to help, because no one else knew that anybody was inside, until your mother's body was found. It was then I knew what this school had done to her, how they tried to hide it. How they had been responsible from the beginning. Your mother had tried to protect our love and me. And I vowed to make those who did this to her pay."

Parker caressed Layna's face.

"And do you know who they were?" he asked. "Oh, the irony. They, darling, were the parents of all your little friends."

Layna's heart sank. It couldn't be.

"Oh yes," Parker clarified, "they went along their merry way, finding regular jobs when they couldn't make it because they either lacked the talent or held on to the guilt of what they had done. Of the secret they all swore to keep hidden. It gave them ulcers. Drove them to drink. Made them overprotective of their little ones. But like so many whose dreams were crushed, they pinned their hopes for fame and fortune onto their children. They couldn't resist enrolling them here. After all, they were legacies, a newfound hope that maybe something good could come of this place, that they could be rescued from the nightmare of the murder they committed. Well, I saw to it that they would never see such respite. You know what they say about the sins of the father and blah, blah, blah."

Layna was stunned. Everything she thought she knew had turned upside down. Her friends were blood related to blood who shed more of the same.

"Doesn't the prank they pulled sound absolutely hilarious?" Dillon asked with a sarcasm that practically cut Layna with its edge.

"About as funny as me coming back at the perfect time," Parker said, "with a new look and life, to finish—"

"You're insane," Layna whispered. Her head had cleared. The time to worry about what had been done, and why, was not now. Maybe it never would be.

"Sticks and stones, honey," Parker muttered.

"You killed so many people. My friends. *My* friends! And all for revenge?"

"Little girl, revenge is overrated. That was part of it, of course. And it felt *good.*" He drew the last word, and it sent a chill through Layna. It was the voice, the cadence of a madman.

"But revenge," Parker went on, his voice rising, "is only as sweet as what you get out of it, and I wanted more. I guess you could say I wanted more than more, but I didn't want just to be selfish. I wanted poetic justice."

Parker rushed toward Layna. Dillon grabbed her face and forced her to look Parker in the eye. "I did this for *you,*" he stated. "So you could be what your mother never was. So you could be what those parents and their disgusting, lazy twits should never have been given the chance to be."

Layna let forth a cry of anguish, a thin string of saliva stretched across her lips.

"Your mother was not supposed to die!" Parker yelled. "She was meant to live. To be one of the important people at Trask. Not another pisher like *them*!" He pointed to the dead bodies in the front row.

"So we did the best thing we could think of," Dillon stated. "We helped Sydney, you know, kill herself, so you could become the star." He loosened his grip on Layna and turned her to face him. "But then we thought, why stop there? Suffer the children. I will admit that Mrs. D., such a beloved teacher, was, I'm sorry to say, collateral damage." Dillon caressed Layna's cheek as she fought the urge to recoil. "We didn't want her to start asking the wrong questions. Or for God's sake, telling you the truth."

Layna faced Parker. She was free from Dillon's hold, but stuck between the two of them.

"Now," Parker said, "the idea to bring you to the forefront through your mother's writing worked like a stroke of genius not even I could've imagined."

"Layna," Dillon added, "your mother didn't write the play you found. We did. The idea was hers, but she never got around to it. Not with the teachers breathing down her neck. Not with a baby to take care of. She wanted to take them to task, but couldn't. So we did."

"And you, all of your friends, fell for it hook, line, and sinker," Parker added. "It wasn't our plan to just go around and slice everyone up willy-nilly. No, no, no. This is the *theater*!"

Layna watched as her father faced the auditorium with his arms outstretched, grandstanding as if there were an audience to appreciate this madness.

"Everything's got to be bigger than life. Especially in death. And the icing on the cake?" Parker leaned toward Layna slowly, almost sweetly. "Tonight is the anniversary of your mother's death, eighteen years ago. Poetic? Pathetic? Take your pick."

Layna closed her eyes, rallying deep within. "But why you, Dillon? Why would you help my father do these things? Did you ever care about me? At all?"

When she opened her eyes, Dillon had changed. His face softened, and she saw the look she had seen before. The one that showed he did care. It gave her hope.

"I did. And I still do," Dillon said. "But you're a smart girl. So let me ask you this. Haven't you ever wondered why our romance failed? Petered out after so short a time? I mean, I did it to get close to you. But just close enough. So you would trust me. But, come on, there's only so much drama a guy can take."

"Now, now, don't tease her," Parker said. "Tell her the good part."

Layna had no idea what was coming next.

"Okay," Dillon said. "Let's pretend I could deal with the drama, all the drama. And you sure have a lot of it. But let's face it, most guys can't. So for fun, and isn't all of this fun, let's also pretend you're getting out of here alive."

"I will," Layna said.

"No, you won't," Parker snapped.

"I had to draw the line somewhere," Dillon continued. "I have to say you were pretty aggressive for a good girl, whatever that means these days. I had to stop things from getting too hot and heavy. I had to tell you that more than a few light pecks were going to lead down a road that the two of us might not be ready for. After all, you're—"

"No," Layna said. She stepped back, felt lightheaded. Parker stopped her.

Dillon nodded. He smiled sickly. "My sister."

Layna crumpled, stunned.

"Don't be upset," Dillon said. "It's not like we went full *Game of Thrones* or anything. I mean, yech."

"It's true," Parker added. "Though I loved your mother, a man has needs. Dillon's mother is, was—well, I'm not really sure. It didn't last. And Dillon here wasn't planned, but I'd say he turned out to be quite a fine, young man."

"Being half-related counts for something, right?" Dillon asked. "But not taste. I mean, Max? *Max*?"

Layna longed for her boyfriend. She wondered whether he was even alive. She closed her eyes and could see him, feel him, smell him. Where was he? What had they done to him?

"Jesus, seeing you with him was enough to make me retch," Dillon said. "If only he were here to see you in this pretty little spot. To see you wriggle like a worm on a hook. Oh. Wait!"

"I have a surprise for my little girl," Parker said. He grabbed Layna's chin in a way she thought he must have deemed loving.

Dillon moved to the right wing of the theater and pulled on a lever to release a rope lock. Layna heard the rushing noise before she saw something race toward them from above. She looked up, shielded herself with her arms, and screamed.

But it stopped before hitting the stage floor just feet in front of them. The two men smirked and then laughed at her reaction.

Max's body, tied with fly ropes. He looked like a dead puppet on strings.

Layna ran to him, devastated. "Max! Max, oh God, no!"

Dillon tugged on the ropes, forcing Max's limp body to stir like a terrifying, dead automaton.

Max lifted his head of his own accord ever so slightly. His eyes fluttered open and shut and open and shut before closing again in fits and starts of consciousness.

"Max, baby, I'm here! Wake up!" Layna pleaded.

Dillon grabbed Max's slack face and shook it. Pretending to be Max, he said in a mocking, squealing voice, "Don't worry, Layna. I don't mind that you tried to get into your brother's pants."

Layna screamed, "Don't you touch him, you son of a bitch!"

Dillon's face turned sour. He threw Max aside. "Don't worry, sweetheart, loverboy will get his."

A darkness glazed over Layna as she furrowed her brow and looked at Dillon. She didn't think about Parker. She focused only on Dillon, and the sickness that had to be coursing through him. The awful things he had said. The twisted lies he had told. She thought of how much he hated Max, how much Max had hated him. Max had sensed something way down deep within Dillon, something he could not articulate but knew was real. If only Layna had listened.

She collected herself, gathering every molecule of resolve she had available. "You know what?" she asked, staring at—through—Dillon.

He leaned in close and smiled a sick, all-knowing smile, ready for Layna's words.

"So will you!" She practically spit at Dillon, at the same time forcing her knee into his groin as hard as she could. She hoped it was powerful enough to render him barren.

His face told her he could taste the pain, sour and pungent. He reeled, fell to his knees, and screamed.

Layna's anger and fear mixed into a highly combustible rush of adrenaline. She ran from her captors.

Parker yelled to his son. "Dammit, get up and get her!" He looked around the theater, frantic.

Dillon stood slowly as Layna hurried into the shadows. "Get back here, you twisted bitch!" he yelled in a broken, strained voice.

Layna acted out of instinct now. She raced down the stage stairs, past the dead audience, and up the aisle, telling herself not to look back at the people she had grown to love. When she reached the doors of the theater, she found them chained shut.

She yanked on them, as if her will could snap the thick, metal links. She turned when she heard Parker's voice and saw his shadow slinking toward her.

"Some children never learn," he said.

Layna slid against the front wall, then back down a far aisle toward a thick, blue construction tarp. As she tightened her body to slip behind it, she saw Dillon on the move, too. A little slower, but moving nonetheless.

It was dark and hot under the thick plastic. Although it blew gently in the breeze, she saw her frenzied breath also caused it to flutter outward, then back, then out again. She closed her eyes and tried to manage the effects of her physical exertion. She remembered an exercise D'Arcangelo had taught her, so she concentrated on the sounds of the tarp before her, the sounds in the auditorium, then, trying even harder, she focused only on sounds outside the building, lilting through the jagged, unfinished roof. Little drops of rain danced and sang before they splotched onto targets below. It calmed her as much as it saddened her, forcing her to recall her favorite teacher.

The noise of Dillon's skulking forced Layna to open her eyes and focus. She spied a wrench on the ground, silently crouched down just enough to reach it, and snatched it up. The metal was heavy and cool in her hand.

"Gonna get you," Dillon threatened in a husky whisper that Layna had never before heard him use. She thought he sounded like a monster—then realized he was a monster.

Dillon's voice was close, mere inches from Layna on the other side of the tarp. The wind moved it once again, sending out a small symphony of crinkles.

"Just find her, for Christ's sakes!" Parker snapped from a distance.

As the tarp ebbed and flowed with the breeze, Layna saw Dillon's feet every time the plastic fluttered out. It was going to be a problem if he looked down.

On the floor, just past where the wrench had lain, she saw a measuring tape. It was too far for her to pick up, and even if it were close, she wouldn't dare reach for it. But she had to do something to distract Dillon, to force him away from her before he took the chance and pulled back the plastic.

So she took a chance and kicked the tape across the floor.

Dillon glanced toward the noise.

Exactly as Layna had hoped.

"Hey!" she yelled from behind the plastic.

Dillon gasped, and Layna heard that he was scared. He didn't have time to react before he was overcome in a sea of blue plastic as Layna pushed forward.

Dillon screamed as he hit the ground, thrashing to twist himself free. Layna raised the wrench high over her head—

"No!" Parker yelled, racing toward Layna from across the room.

Layna brought the wrench down hard. She did not know where she hit him, but Dillon yelped in pain. Still, he wriggled under her, getting one of his legs free. Then an arm. Layna closed her eyes and threw the wrench down onto Dillon again, this time where she believed his head might be. There was a thick crunch. Dillon went limp. Parker continued to take huge, frightening strides toward her.

Layna dashed into the darkness, heading back to the stage, as Parker approached the motionless Dillon. Parker pulled the tarp away and looked down at his son, very much dead. Blood was already pooling beneath the boy's head, and Parker let out a wretched scream that seemed to shake dust from the rafters.

"You killed my son!" Parker yelled to Layna, to the building, to anyone.

The words hit Layna hard. She would remember her father's scream, and those words, forever. They would haunt her. If she got out alive, even on days when the horrors of this campus were a distant memory, and she saw the faces of her friends as if through fogged glass, she would be shaken by the sound.

She was a murderer. And she would have to live with that, because being a killer was the only way to live, she would tell herself.

Parker scanned the auditorium. He charged toward the stage, angry, yelling, "I'll kill you slow! I did this for you!"

Layna's voice filled the air. "You did this for you!" She was sure Parker couldn't see her though the flapping plastic, shadowed saw horses, and other work materials.

"You did nothing but destroy innocent lives," Layna shouted out to him. Her anger seemed to subside, and her voice took on a more sallow, somber note.

"Liar, liar, pants on fire," Parker stated. "I loved your mother and I loved you. Now get out here, you damn little bitch!"

Layna darted about, keeping an eye on Parker. He flitted left and right and back and forth at her shadow, or the flapping fabric. She took satisfaction in his confusion.

"What's the matter? Can't catch me?" she taunted.

Parker passed the orchestra pit and took measured steps onto the stage. He looked around, slow, his head cocked, listening for Layna. He was near the ghost light in the center of the stage, but saw nothing. Then he began whistling a sing-songy tune.

"Come out, come out, wherever you are," he taunted.

Layna made her move. She appeared to rise from the orchestra pit, looking like nothing more than a silhouette as the ghost light blinded Parker.

Parker put his hands up to shield his eyes and took a step away from the light. He smiled as Layna came into clearer view. "Now that's my little—"

He stopped when he saw she did not have a wrench in her

hands.

Layna instead held tight to Parker's Glock. With two steady hands, she pointed directly at his chest. She didn't know the weapon like he did, but she knew the hammer was partially cocked and the trigger needed little pressure to fire. He raised his hands.

"You should have worked a little harder on the manuscript. Done a little more research," Layna said. "Step on a crack, walk under a ladder, a rabbit's foot. Those are the easy ones. But, wouldn't you know, it's bad luck to whistle in a theater."

Parker's expression fell.

"You want drama?" Layna asked calmly. "You got it."

She fired.

Parker took three shots, each hitting his chest higher than the last. The force of the recoil caused Layna to raise the gun each time. She watched as her father's body flew backward onto the stage, landing in a pile of plastic, metal, and tools. He contorted into the plastic until he was covered with it from head to toe. She shuffled closer to him and saw blood trickling onto the stage.

She kicked the body. No breathing. No movement. Things grew hazy, until she heard Max stirring in the darkness behind her.

"Oh, God, Max! Max, talk to me!" she said. She rushed over to him, dropping the gun. She frantically tried to undo the thick ropes that kept him floating above the floor of the stage.

Max cleared his throat, but when the words came, it sounded as if he had swallowed sand. "Nice shooting, babe."

Layna smiled, even as she cried, and worked her shaking fingers feverishly to free her boyfriend.

But a subtle and unexpected rattle from behind forced her to turn. She saw nothing, then looked up at Max, still weaving in and out of an unconscious daze. Layna stopped fiddling with the ropes and bent down to pick up the gun. The rattle came from where her father had gone down. She stepped as if her feet were trudging through molasses, wondering if he had stirred. If, maybe, he wasn't dead.

Standing above the tarp, she waited. Waited for another movement or another sound. She kicked the plastic. Then the metal. The tools.

They scattered effortlessly and her stomach turned. Her heart exploded in a flutter of beats. She pulled the covering away.

No body.

Thin trails of blood dripped down a set of rickety, wooden steps. Steps that led through a trapdoor in the stage and, Layna presumed, out into the world. Shocked and confused and sad and afraid, Layna looked back at Max. She looked at the bodies of her friends. And then she looked down at the swinging trap door.

This time there were tears. Too many to count. They came freely and fell into the darkness below, a darkness that left everything uncertain.

EPILOGUE

One year later

Lightning and thunder did their intricate dance as rain reflected the light of an off-Broadway marquee.

JINXED!
A New Thriller

Playbills and images teased the production as a murder mystery in two acts, written by Amanda & Layna Kincaid.

Inside the theater, a comfortable but less than well-appointed space, the ninety-nine seats were mostly filled with college students on break, adults looking for something off the beaten path, and a few critics hoping to use their witticisms in reviews, whether good or bad. The audience sat silently, some with mouths agape, as the play climaxed.

On stage, Layna was rested and strong, though she looked tired and haggard, thanks to makeup and costume. She was pointing a gun at a man, older, strapping and strong, dressed in a coat that screamed detective. Or police officer.

But in this moment of art imitating life, he was Father.

Layna closed her eyes, and though no one in the audience knew it, she was not acting so much as remembering. The feel of the trigger, what the gun was about to do.

Layna's character spoke. "Looks like you don't need a broken mirror for bad luck," she said, though the words were slightly different when it counted. When it really was life and death.

The fake gun fired at Detective Craven, and Layna recalled that the real object had a thrust and a force that slapped her back. The plastic prop in her hand would do no real damage. The actor playing her character's father hit the floor.

But this time he stayed very dead. There was no trap door.

Only the one in Layna's memory.

She turned to the audience, ending the performance with one word. The summation of what led her to this moment, a time bathed in truths, lies, bad luck, and blood.

"Jinx," she whispered.

The lights went out, the curtain fell, and Layna heard the applause she had longed for as a reward for the gauntlet she had endured.

When the lights came back and the curtain lifted, Layna and the cast gave their final bows. She smiled appreciatively, looking into the audience, trying to connect with as many of them as she could. But if she were being honest, she was searching for faces that reminded her of those she had lost on her journey here, Sydney's and Alice's and Nancy's and Crosby's.

She also thought of Dillon's. And her father's.

Layna had come to terms with the sad notion that, no matter how she wished, they would never be hers again.

The curtain fell, and with it, her daydreams of old friends. Layna welcomed a throng of hugs, kisses, and thank yous from other cast and the crew, but her perfunctory smile transformed into one of real feeling when she saw the one person who was true and good. And hers.

Max. He grabbed her, held her tight, and kissed her deep. She felt wrapped in safety, in warmth, in love.

"You clean up real nice, Mr. Reynolds," Layna said, admiring his gray suit.

"It's not every night my girl has an opening," he said.

"And? It was good?" she asked, she hoped.

Max rolled his eyes up. "Good? Nah. Perfect, like you. You should be proud."

"They didn't come, did they?" Layna asked, thinking of her grandparents.

Max shook his head. "Give them time. A lot's happened between the three of you."

She reached up on the tips of her toes and kissed him before the two made their way backstage to her dressing room among the commotion of people talking and greeting, absorbed in the throng of a successful opening.

The noise grew louder when two teenagers, a boy and a girl, rushed around the corner of the hallway. Layna jumped back when they ran into her.

"Hey!" Max yelled.

Layna instinctively stepped behind Max, but she felt somewhat foolish when she saw that the girl simply held an autograph book, and the boy had flowers. Petals fell to the ground from the accidental collision.

"OMG, super sorry!" the girl screeched, giddy with excitement.

The boy thrust the flowers toward Layna, who had no choice but to accept them with a smile.

"That's all right," she said. "Thank you, these are very pretty."

The boy blushed and the girl stepped forward, practically pushing Max out of the way. "You are, like, totally my hero."

"Heroine," the boy corrected with a nudge of his elbow.

"Whatevs," the girl replied.

Max and Layna shared a wry smile.

"I'm gonna go get the car," Max said. "You good?"

"Yeah," Layna said. "I got this."

Layna watched Max leave. He turned at one point to wave his

finger by his head, suggesting the kids were crazy.

Layna giggled, winked at him, and then turned her attention back to her fans.

"Can I have your autograph?" the girl asked.

Layna took the pen and started to sign.

"You are so awesome. I can't believe you went to Trask!" the boy blurted out.

"We so wanna go there. We'd do anything to be famous like you!" the girl admitted.

"*Anything*," the boy emphasized. It caught Layna off guard. The intensity. The desire, the need.

The desperation, she thought.

Layna felt the pen in her hand slipping. Suddenly she felt alone, even though there were two people fawning over her, a crowd of theatergoers chatting about her performance, and Max waiting for her outside.

She handed the signed book back to the girl. "There you go. Thanks for coming. Goodnight."

The boy and girl skipped off. Layna watched them disappear around the corner, thinking back to when she was just like them, with an idol and a dream, even a need. But they would never know the price she paid.

Layna was now in the hallway alone, and the voices in the building subsided. She shook off the feeling and walked to her dressing room.

As she entered, she shut the door behind her and leaned against it. Flowers and congratulatory notes were strewn about the modest room. "We did it, Mom," she said aloud, smiling as she went to her mirror and looked at it. Melancholy enveloped her. She had tried to shake the feeling for the past year, but could not. Maybe never would.

More than her face reflected back from the surface of the

mirror, which was plastered with pictures. Some of the cast, but mostly of her old friends, Max, Crosby, Nancy, and Alice. Even Mrs. D'Arcangelo. And, of course, her mother. She would never forget them, couldn't. She wouldn't let herself.

Layna sat down and pulled the school photo of her mother from the mirror. The pretty young woman was sitting on a bench at Trask, outside the theater. Layna wondered who had taken the picture, how many friends her mother had, and how much she loved the daughter she had kept hidden away in secret.

When Layna looked back up to the mirror, she saw, in the place where the photo had been, a reflected view of a vase of flowers sitting across the room. It was a large, ornate bouquet that sat on a chair next to an armoire. Layna wrinkled her brow when she saw them, as if she had not seen them before.

Layna turned quickly, as if they might disappear. She got up to get a closer look. They were beautiful. Colorful, airy and exotic.

Up close she saw that they were not flowers at all, but feathers. Peacock feathers, and their eyes were all staring at her. Unnerved, she picked up the small card attached to them. Flipping it open, she read the typed message inside:

I know they're bad luck inside a theater …
But I just had to "see" you.

A feeling she had hoped never to feel again crept over her in dark tingles that started at the base of her back. She flipped the card over and saw, written in ink:

Love,
Dad

Layna dropped the card in horror. It fluttered to the ground.

In those fleeting seconds, illuminated by fits and spurts of electric blue from the now raging storm outside, the armoire door opened.

The last thing Layna saw was the twisted mask, comedy and tragedy lunging at her together, even as she tried to scream.

About the Author

Thommy Hutson is an award-winning screenwriter, producer, director, and author who is considered the foremost authority on *A Nightmare on Elm Street*. A graduate of UCLA, Thommy has written and produced critically acclaimed genre projects such as *Never Sleep Again: The Elm Street Legacy*, *Inside Story: Scream*, *More Brains! A Return to the Living Dead*, and *Crystal Lake Memories: The Complete History of Friday the 13th*. Thommy was born and raised in New York but now resides in the mountains of Southern California.

Follow Thommy on Twitter: @ThommyHutson

www.thommyhutson.com

52966837R00144

Made in the USA
Middletown, DE
23 November 2017